Splintered North

ANNA KATMORE

We thought we had forever together.

But *forever* was a long time coming.

1. Heartbeats

The room is a cocoon of darkness, pierced only by the glow of blue light spilling from the monitors surrounding me. Cool air whispers through a tube and into my nostrils, a steady rhythm in sync with the soft beeping accompanying my every breath.

A cuff clings to my left upper arm, squeezing and releasing in odd intervals. My feet are toasty, but my hands are cold and abandoned. I long to tuck them under the blanket, but for some reason, I can't manage. My mouth won't open either, leaving me unable to ask the girl for even a glass of water as she drifts to my bedside, sweeping an unfamiliar device across my forehead. I can only stare into her eyes as she offers me a warm smile. This isn't the first time. She's been here before. Has she left at all? How long have I been imprisoned in this room?

My gaze lingers on her as she circles the bed, inspecting the monitors before plucking a strip of paper from one. She examines it, then reaches for a suspended bottle, a tube snaking from it to my hand. Again, our eyes connect, and her gentle smile returns.

Dressed in white pants and a form-fitting yellow tee, she sports earrings adorned with tiny, vibrant metal feathers. Her jet-black hair, edgy and short, frames her face. I don't know her, or why she's here, but I'm grateful for her presence. She's like a Woodstock-era fairy godmother. Everyone needs one, right? I yearn to reciprocate her smile, but my face remains frozen. My eyes are the only part of me that can follow her. A sudden chill creeps into the back of my hand, and my eyelids grow heavy.

*

The moment my eyes flutter open, I search for my yellow-clad fairy. Relief washes over me when I find her across the room, scribbling in a folder. Outside the window, darkness reigns, but inside, blue light bathes the room like an icy grotto.

I observe her, wondering why she doesn't sit or what she's even documenting. I long to ask, but my parched throat and aching jaw prevent any sound. In fact, my entire face throbs with pain. I close my mouth and struggle to recall the cause. A fight, perhaps?

Faint images plague my mind.

Dark shapes...

Was I battling with a bear?

It sounds absurd, but the memory is vivid, if somewhat blurred...with snow.

In the beams of headlights.

Of North's car—

The memory sends a jolt through my body, and I gasp for air. The once-peaceful beeping above accelerates, mimicking a ticking bomb counting down. My good fairy whirls around as I attempt to sit up, cables and tubes straining against my movement. In an instant, she's at my side, her delicate hands on my shoulders, gently easing me back onto the pillow. How can someone barely five-foot-five be so strong?

"Where's North?" I rasp, hardly audible. Desperation floods my eyes as I search hers, needing her to grasp the urgency. The frantic beeping intensifies.

"Everything's okay, Adrian," she attempts to reassure me, but her expression betrays her words. "You need to rest now."

Reality slams into me as I recognize my surroundings.

The entire evening, the car ride, the accident—brutal images flash through my mind.

The young nurse eyes me sympathetically and reaches for the IV bag of clear liquid hanging next to my bed. But this time, I grip her hand before she can adjust the flow and knock me out again. "Please!" I beg, my voice cracking with the effort. "You have to help me." She's my fairy godmother, after all.

The young woman silences the incessant beeping of the monitor above me. Did she just turn off my heart?

"I need to see North Beckett. Please!" I implore her again. "He was in the car with me. Is he okay? Is he in the hospital, too?"

I'm not sure how much she understood of my slurred mumbling, but she takes my hand and lets out a slow breath, as if stalling for time. "I'm afraid I can't—"

Her words are cut off by a different voice that grabs my attention.

"Adrian?"

The voice comes from the hallway, where the door is ajar. "Adrian!" it calls again, excitement evident. A moment later, Ruth bursts in and rushes to my side. She clasps my right hand, an oxygen monitor clipped to my index finger, and presses it to her lips. Her face is stained with tears, her eyes red and swollen. She looks awful, the picture of grief...

A knot forms in my throat, making it difficult to breathe. "What happened to him?" I whisper.

"I'm so relieved you're awake, my dear!" she sobs

into my hand. "The doctor said you have a concussion and severe bruising, but you'll heal."

"Please, Ruth!" I try to snap her out of her tears, removing the bulky monitor from my finger. Holding both her hands, I press them to my chest, forcing her to look at me. "Tell me what happened to North."

Finally, understanding flickers in her eyes. And boundless compassion. For me? She frees one hand from my grasp and tenderly brushes my check, as gentle as a feather. No wonder she's sympathetic. After slamming into the airbag, I must look like I've been hit by a truck.

"North is—"

"Ma'am," the nurse with the quirky feather earrings cuts her off, stepping beside her and placing a hand on her shoulder. "He needs to rest now. And you should, too. You're not even supposed to be in here."

"Yes—yes, of course," Ruth stammers, allowing herself to be guided towards the door without further protest.

"No! Ruth! Please!" Desperate, I stretch my arms out to her, lacking the strength to lift my body from the bed. "Tell me what happened!"

As she turns back to look at me one last time, her expression becomes vacant, as if she's drugged and incapable of making decisions for herself. The raven-haired fairy supports her empathetically and guides her out.

"Ruth!" My pitiful cry echoes in my empty room,

and I squeeze my eyes shut, heart aching.

It takes torturous minutes for the girl in the yellow T-shirt to return. Alone. Helplessly, I watch her cross the room. She's probably in her mid-twenties, but she moves through this world as if she's been working at this hospital her whole life. She circles my bed, looking at me like someone who just intentionally destroyed a continent but had no other choice. She's well aware of the pain she's caused me. It's only a simple piece of information that could alleviate my despair, yet people like her think they know better and can decide what's best for someone else.

Fuck it! She knows nothing at all!

With her shoulders hanging from the weight of guilt, she approaches me and offers a glass of water, straw sticking out like some sort of olive branch. It's not enough to erase her betrayal, but I grudgingly accept, taking a feeble sip without tearing my gaze from her deep brown eyes.

"Stop looking at me like that," she pleads, her sigh barely audible. "I can't give you any answers."

"You could've let Ruth tell me," I retort, drained. She was my freaking fairy godmother, for Christ's sake!

"You need some sleep. You've been through hell." She turns her back to me, setting the glass down on the nightstand, way too far for me to reach.

But I'm not done fighting. "Either tell me what happened to North now," I rasp, my voice weaker than I'd like, but still managing to sit up, "or I'll rip these tubes out and go find him myself."

She faces me again, the file from earlier in her grasp. "If you do that, I'll have to sedate you, and you'll be out 'til the afternoon. Is that what you want?" Despite my weakness, she appears hesitant, standing frozen before me, clutching the file to her chest as if pleading for me to back down willingly.

Desperate, I prop myself up on one arm and give her a beseeching look. "Please—" I'm at a loss. "I only want to know if he's still breathing."

For a moment, she bites her lip and exhales sharply. Then, unexpectedly, she crosses the room and shuts the door. As she inches closer and perches on the edge of the bed, she murmurs, her voice soothing as if to mend a wound, "You both arrived in the ER four hours ago, but they only brought you here to the ICU."

I feel like I've slammed into a brick wall at 120 mph. My lungs constrict, and as the blood pressure cuff on my arm starts to inflate again, I tense my muscles and fight against it, as if my life depends on it. "What does that mean?" I stammer, the words cracking in my throat.

The nurse clutches the file on her lap, placing her free hand on my clenched fist. "There were major complications, and they had to resuscitate him multiple times. That's all we know for now."

Complications. *"Still no pulse,"* the haunting words

reverberate in my ears.

"The rod in his chest..." I mumble, my gaze darting around the room, frantically seeking something solid, something to erase the horrific image from my mind. But there's nothing. "So I've been lying here, high on painkillers and delirious, while North is still fighting for his life—"

Or he may have already lost the battle.

Dear God, no! I squeeze my eyes shut, choking back a sob. This can't be real. It just can't!

"There's nothing you can do right now. It's best if you lie down and let the meds do their thing," she says, rising to adjust the drip on the IV bag. The liquid courses through the vein in the back of my hand, icy cold.

Defeated, I let the girl guide me back onto the pillow. It's like the air has been vacuumed from my lungs, and I'm drowning in the debris of my broken world.

And what about North's grandma?

"Ruth?" I ask, more absent already than feeling anchored in reality. "How long has she been here?"

"She got here just after you did, with a friend. He was first on the scene and called for help." The nurse leans over the bed to reattach the clip to my index finger. "We've tried to get a doctor to speak with her twice," she admits, likely bending some hospital rules by sharing this with me, "but no one's shown up yet. She received a mild sedative from us earlier and is resting in the nurses' room.

Her friend's still with her, but I should check on her soon."

I watch her wearily as she moves toward the door and places her hand on the handle. But before she can leave me alone, I ask in a whisper, "What's your name?"

Glancing back, she gifts me with the warm smile I first saw when she welcomed me back to consciousness. "Marie."

Marie. I consider if it's a suitable name for a good fairy. And I decide it's perfect. "Thanks, Marie..." I rasp.

She nods and promises, "I'll be right back."

Whether she keeps her promise or not, I don't notice, because the painkillers soon drag me into a fog of indifference, and I sink into dreamless slumber.

Next, I wake up to the hushed conversation between two women by my bedside, one gently stroking my hand. I fight to open my eyes, vaguely recognizing Ruth's face before me. She looks exhausted. I wish I could get up and give her my bed.

"Hey...how are you?" I murmur weakly.

She lets out a deep sigh, visibly moved, pressing my hand to her face and kissing my knuckles. "My dear boy," she merely chokes out, likely because she can't bring herself to admit she's never felt as horrible in her life as she does tonight.

Same here.

"Has a doctor been here?" I ask Marie, who's

perched on a chair against the wall. "Any news?"

She just shakes her head with deep sympathy.

"What time is it?" It's awful, drifting in and out of consciousness, never knowing how long I've been out.

"Half past midnight," she informs me. "You only slept for half an hour." She then stands up and swipes that strange thing across my forehead again. When she checks the display and murmurs, "Ninety-eight point six. Looks good," I realize she's been taking my temperature this whole time. Next, she whips out a small flashlight and shines it into both of my eyes, prying each one open with her fingers. She doesn't comment on what she sees, simply jotting something down in the folder she's been using all night. I turn back to Ruth, who still cradles my hand with tender care.

Suddenly, two deep voices reverberate from the hallway, and a man in his early forties with Asian features strides in. He resembles Lieutenant Sulu from *Star Trek*, if he wore all white and had a stethoscope draped around his neck instead of a Starfleet insignia. "Mrs. Beckett?" he inquires softly.

"Yes?" Ruth blurts out, her hands shaking as she springs up from her chair and faces the doctor.

My heart lodges in my throat as well. Everyone in the room can hear it because, at some point between my last chat with Marie and now, she must have cranked up the monitor above me.

"I'm Dr. Kaito. I understand you haven't been updated on your grandson's condition. Please join me outside for a moment." The doctor's voice is even and controlled, as if he's mastered the art of retrieving people from hospital rooms in the dead of night without revealing whether he bears good or bad news.

But I can't let him take Ruth away. I need to hear what's happening with North, so I tighten my grip on her hand. Ruth immediately returns the pressure and pats my fingers with her other hand. Then she tells the doctor quietly but firmly, "We can talk in here. What's going on with North?"

His serious gaze flickers from her to me and back. "I'm sorry, but we can only disclose information to family members."

Ruth, not even glancing at me, stands her ground by my side. "Adrian is family. He's my grandson, too."

Oh, Ruth...

In that instant, my heart swells with so much love for this woman, I wish it were true.

Dr. Kaito looks momentarily puzzled, likely because he hasn't read anything about it in the medical records, but he accepts the new information without question. Anyway, who is he to decide whether a woman in her seventies could have only one grandchild and no more? "Very well." He grabs a red plastic chair for himself and asks Ruth to sit back down. "Your grandson--North," he adds quickly to avoid confusion, "arrived in the emergency room last night with severe injuries. During the accident, he was impaled by a piece of a wooden pole—a broken snow guidepost."

I hold my breath, but Ruth gasps in horror.

Unfazed by her reaction, the doctor continues. He's clearly used to such responses from family members. "The wood damaged numerous blood vessels and grazed his left lung. Your grandson lost a significant amount of blood and had to be resuscitated at the scene."

Ruth pulls her hands away from me, covering her mouth in shock. Tears spill over again and course down her wrinkled, ashen cheeks. I wish I could hold her. And that she could hold me. Everything inside me clenches as I listen to the story again, one I experienced just hours ago.

"Is he okay now?" Ruth croaks, her voice begging for good news.

But Dr. Kaito doesn't say yes or no. He proceeds in a detached manner, as if he must meticulously cover every page of the medical report—and as if he weren't dealing with traumatized people here. "North was eventually stabilized for transport, but in the emergency room, he suffered another cardiac arrest. The main issue is that a small splinter has entered his left ventricle."

"Oh no!" Ruth's round body quivers as if the entire world is shaking.

I only realize I've been clenching my fists in tension

when warm, gentle fingers cover my left hand. As the doctor finally shows some emotion and places a compassionate hand on Ruth's shoulder, I open my hand for Marie and let her comfort me in this way.

"Your grandson wasn't stable enough for transport to a larger hospital, so we brought in a cardiac specialist from Vancouver. The surgery began just under an hour ago," the doctor continues. "We won't know more until it's over."

If he makes it... Those words hang palpably in the air above us, even though the doctor doesn't voice them aloud.

I can't think clearly as a thousand images race through my mind, all featuring North gravely injured on the operating table, and in one of them, I'm standing at his grave.

"My God!" Ruth exclaims, deeply shaken. At that moment, a second man in his seventies appears in the doorway. Tall, slim, with short gray hair, round metal glasses, and a goatee, he looks erudite, almost like a university professor. "Oh, George!" she cries and runs into his arms.

He embraces her tightly and tenderly, murmuring into her disheveled, pinned-up hair, "Don't worry, Ruthie. North is strong. He'll make it." It's evident he's been eavesdropping from the hallway, but who he is, I haven't a clue.

Dr. Kaito also stands up and approaches the pair, looking Ruth in the eyes. "Your boys were fortunate that Dr. Valentine was the first on the scene. If he hadn't been there and started resuscitation right away, any help would have been too late for North."

Dr. Valentine? *George Alexander?* I don't know what he did in his life to make Ruth so angry at him for years. But the fact that he was a guardian angel for her grandson tonight seems to have mended their relationship.

"The surgery will take several more hours," the doctor tells her. "You should go home and rest for a bit. We'll contact you as soon as there's news." He pats her shoulder in farewell and then turns to me. "Take care," he says, nodding before quietly leaving the room.

For an immeasurable period, all I hear is my own breathing. I hear North's grandmother crying, and I catch snippets of conversation that don't make sense to me right now.

"...heard the doctor... I'll drive you home, you'll sleep a few hours, and tomorrow morning... Come on, Ruthie..."

Dr. Valentine also says a few things to me, but I don't know if I respond or not. Everything feels like an underwater whirlwind. Marie leans over me. The light goes on and off. Ruth squeezes my hand and kisses my forehead.

Then the room falls silent, and all I hear is the

electronic echo of my steady heartbeat as an unbearable eternity opens up in front of me.

"Will he die?" I ask quietly when my blank gaze eventually returns from the depths of the ceiling above me. I don't know where she is in the room, but I can sense she's still here. My good fairy.

Her gentle response comes from the window, surprising me. "What do you believe, Adrian?"

It's an odd question, but I ponder it for a moment. Since I met North, I believe in so many things I never thought possible before. I believe in happiness. In courage. In freedom. In love at first sight. And maybe even a little in... "Destiny."

"Do you want to know what I believe?"

I turn my head toward her and look at her expectantly.

"I've been working at this hospital for a while now, and I've seen my fair share of miracles. I truly believe that if someone wants to live badly enough, they'll find a way." She circles my bed and plops down into the red vinyl chair with metal legs where Ruth had been sitting earlier. "Your grandma filled me in on some of North's life while you were out. Hockey, good friends who care about him—you know, the works. I bet he's one of those people who really want to live."

Her words wrap around me like a comforting hug.

"Get some more rest. I'll let you know if there's any

more news, promise."

Because I trust her, I let myself drift back to sleep. When I wake again, my head feels clearer and I can even read the clock above the door. It's four in the morning.

Marie is still in the chair beside me, but now she's got a book in hand, her feet propped up on a second chair. My stirring must have changed my heartbeat because she looks first at the monitor, then into my eyes. "Hey," she greets warmly, smiling like she always does when I emerge from the darkness. She closes her book, rises, silences my heart monitor, and brings a glass of water with a straw to my bedside.

I take a grateful sip and wait for her to sit back down before asking, "Is the ward usually this quiet during the holidays, or is there another reason you're able to spend so much time with me?"

Marie laughs softly like a real fairy would. "We're just a small hospital, and we don't usually have many intensive care patients. Tonight, it's just Rachel and me here, and you're our only patient." She shoots me a teasing grin. "I drew the short straw, so here I am."

"Nice," I reply, my tone gently dipped in sarcasm. Still, I appreciate her attempt to lift my spirits and her company. "Any news?" I demand, concern creeping back into my voice.

The good fairy shakes her head, but this time she seems determined to keep my mind off my worries and my fear for North. She effortlessly steers our conversation towards movies, and soon enough, we're debating the merits of film adaptations of famous novels. We're on the same page with *The Lord of the Rings*, but we butt heads over various Stephen King adaptations. She brings up a few other titles I'm not familiar with, neither the books nor the movies.

When she goes on to share her experience training as an ICU nurse, it sounds grueling. A lot of her classmates dropped out of the course. Not everyone has what it takes to be a good fairy, I guess. Just as I mention that my mom works in a hospital, too, the automatic doors in the hallway whoosh open, interrupting our conversation at 5:30 in the morning.

My heart skips a beat, and I hold my breath. Maybe a doctor has some good news about the surgery. *Please, let it be good news!*

As Marie gets up and peers into the illuminated hallway, I fix my gaze on the open door. Who's out there? What does she see?

"We're bringing in a patient from ER Three. Male. Car accident," a soft voice says, not really addressing Marie.

"What's his name?" another woman asks. That must be Rachel, the other nurse on the ward whom I haven't met yet. I nearly bite through my cheek, waiting for the answer.

"Carlton Hayes."

My hope soars, only to be crushed as my world crumbles around me. Marie looks at me sympathetically. "We'll just have to wait a bit longer," she tries to reassure me, moving closer. "Don't give up hope now."

Easier said than done.

"Okay. Room One is taken. Put him in Room Two," Rachel directs the new arrival in the hallway. "You can hook him up to the monitor right away."

A bed rolls past my room, but I can't see the patient because one of the three blue-clad resident doctors walks alongside, flipping through a clipboard. She's the one with the soft voice, and just before she vanishes behind the next wall, she says, "No, wait. Hayes was the doctor who performed the surgery. It was entered incorrectly here."

I bolt upright in bed, held back by the thin plastic tube beneath my nose connected to an oxygen tank behind the headboard. I yank it from my face—I can barely breathe with or without it at this point.

Mechanical noises emanate from the next room as the bed is locked into place. "His name is—"

Please, let it be him!

"North Beckett."

And then there's a sound that triggers a tidal wave of emotions inside me, which I can only express as two solitary tears. The rhythmic beeping of a heart monitor.

2. A time without dreams

"Help me up, Marie."

"No way, Adrian. You know it's too soon," Marie scolds me, turning her back to me by the window.

"I need to see him, please! I just have to!" I hate feeling this helpless, begging for something that should be my right.

The doctors who took North to the ICU left about twenty minutes ago, and Rachel, the redhead with wild curls, has just finished getting him settled. She told Marie she's taking a break to grab breakfast for them both. Now's my chance!

"Even if I wanted to, I couldn't let you see him,"

Marie fires back. "It's not visiting hours, and you're not even related."

I'm sure the first part doesn't matter since I'm not exactly a visitor here. And as for the other part... "You heard earlier that we're related. Same grandmother." That should count for something, right? "So, we're—"

I draw a blank, my concussion and growing panic clouding my thoughts. She smirks, raising an eyebrow in challenge.

Damn it, think! "Brothers," I blurt out, seizing the first thing that comes to mind.

"Brothers? Sure." Marie nearly laughs. "Guess you always call your grandmother by her first name, then?"

Ugh.

Since she's still pretending to be too busy with my chart to deal with me, I go for the jugular. "If North has another cardiac arrest"—*God forbid!*—"and doesn't make it, it'll be on you if I couldn't be with him."

Finally, she abandons the chart and stomps to the foot of my bed, glaring daggers at me. The good fairy in the yellow T-shirt can't pull off a seriously mad expression, though. "That's low," she growls, hands on her hips.

"I know. So...will you help me, or should I just crawl over there?"

She lets out a frustrated sigh, then rolls her eyes. "Fine." Marie disconnects me from the machines and IV, then switches off the monitor. "Stay put," she orders before vanishing into the hallway, only to reappear with a wheelchair.

As she helps me out of bed, I realize how weak my legs feel. My head swims, and my knees shake. I tug at my hospital gown, grateful I still have my boxers on to save me from flashing my goods on this little adventure.

Carefully, Marie aids me with the wheelchair and then pushes me out of the room. With each passing second, my heart races faster. We're just a few steps away, then finally heading through a frosted-glass door marked with a giant '2.' North's heartbeat echoes through the entire ward, lonely and sorrowful. The haunting rhythm tightens my throat.

As Marie stops just short of his bed, each breath becomes a battle, like trying to survive in the bone-chilling Antarctic cold. I carefully plant my bare feet on the sterile linoleum floor and push myself up from the wheelchair. My fairy is there for support, but she can't shield me from the heartache of seeing North, motionless and hooked to a ventilator.

His lips are sealed with white adhesive, holding the tube in place. The pump in the glass cylinder rises and falls in sync with North's chest. Instead of a hospital gown, his bare upper body lies exposed, with only a white bandage concealing the evidence of his surgery.

I take a step closer, my own body numb. He's connected to monitors and IVs, and so much more.

Infusions from a bottle and two plastic bags. A container draining blood from his wound. A tube attached to a port in his neck, controlled by a computer. I thought my room was high-tech, but this feels like the command center of a spaceship.

"What's all this for?" I ask Marie, my voice shaking.

"They're probably keeping him in a deep sleep for now," she explains softly. "After major procedures, it helps the healing process when patients can't move. When North wakes up in a few days, the worst will be behind him. Trust me, it's for the best."

A few days? I swallow hard, feeling a cold shiver run down my spine. Her attempt at reassurance can't hide the truth: his condition is still critical.

"He's not out of the woods yet, is he?"

She hesitates before answering honestly, "No. Not yet."

Gently, I take North's hand, resting on the blanket. It's warm but lifeless, as if he were already—

For a moment, I squeeze my eyes shut, pushing the thought away. He's alive! That's all that matters for now.

Looking at his bruised and battered face again, I wonder if not coming back to Canada early could have prevented this. If I'd stayed in Oakspeak for the holidays, he'd be tending to the horses, playing with Chester in the hayloft, and sharing chocolate cookies with his grandmother.

But now...he's trapped in a sleep no thunderclap could rouse him from. And it's all my fault.

As tears blur my vision, I sniffle and wipe my wet cheeks. Swallowing the pain, I intertwine my fingers with his, carefully curling them to mimic his grasp. It's not the same, but it's something.

"Is he dreaming?" I whisper, staring at his closed eyes, searching for a flicker of movement—anything. But there's nothing.

"No. Anesthesia suppresses those brain centers."

The thought leaves a heavy ache in my chest. "So, he'll just lie in the dark for days?" All alone...maybe terrified...

"He's not aware of any of this, Adrian," Marie assures me, her eyes filled with empathy. "To him, it's like no time has passed between now and when you two last saw each other in the car."

The idea offers a strange sense of comfort. I cling to it, like a lifeline, as I hope and pray he'll make it through the coming days.

That he'll survive and come back to me.

He's my North Star! He has to return and shine for me again!

My left leg buckles, but Marie catches me before I tumble onto North's bed, which would be disastrous.

"Come on," she insists. "I'll take you back to your

bed. You can visit him again later when you're stronger."

This time, I don't fight her. She helps me into the wheelchair and pushes me back to my room where she silently reconnects me to the machines and tucks me in. Then she places a hand on my forearm, her voice gentle. "Are you alright?"

The question cuts deep. But I can't talk right now, so I nod and close my eyes. I'm exhausted and spent. The only thing I want to do is sleep...as long as North does. So that, in a few days, we can wake up together and finally hold each other again.

*

These are the darkest days of my life. I grow stronger while North lies motionless, hour by hour, unable to breathe on his own.

Ruth visits the hospital daily, sometimes with Dr. George Alexander Valentine, sometimes alone. We stand by North's bed for hours or sit in my room, talking or lost in silence.

After my first night in the ICU, I called my mom and shared part of the story. Not wanting her to worry, I told her I'd spent a night in the hospital but was going home afterward. She doesn't need to know the full extent of North's injuries. Maybe someday I'll tell her, when this nightmare is just a memory.

Sandy heard the whole story but swore not to reveal it until I'm ready. Her heart-wrenching sobs over the phone were unbearable, and my heart broke all over again.

Marie worked two more nights before switching to day shifts. During that time, she spent many hours with me.

Today, on the first day of the new year, I'm discharged, and she hugs me goodbye, even though we know we'll see each other again soon. Because North is still deeply sedated.

Returning to the farm feels strange, without the constant hum of the ICU. I miss North and the ability to visit him whenever I want. But the worst part is not hearing his heartbeat at night. It's like I've left a piece of myself behind at the hospital. The best part of my life.

While I was gone, Dean Harris, the neighboring farmer's son, and Madelyn kindly tended to the horses. Once I've fully recovered, I take over the stable duties, giving them a break. Everything else can wait, as Ruth and I drive to the hospital daily after lunch, spending as much time with North as they allow. Occasionally, Maddie joins us, but she can't enter the ICU.

By now, she's informed the university that North won't be returning for some time. She's also reached out to his friends through Facebook, explaining what happened, and shared the outpouring of heartfelt messages and well-wishes posted on his profile with me. I don't see them myself since we aren't even friends on Facebook. When she sees my shoulder slumping with the pressure of sorrow, Maddie persuades me to come ice skating with her. She knows that North had started teaching me before Christmas and wants to give me some extra lessons to take my mind off of the hospital for a couple of hours.

It's nice of her, and I force myself to gift her a couple of smiles on the frozen lake.

Time seems to blur as the cold days pass, and my only hope is for North to wake up. A few extra nights of sleep stretch into a week, then ten days, and soon, sixteen. It feels as if someone has pushed me into the abyss of hell and closed the door for good.

But then, one Wednesday morning, there's finally a ray of hope. If his vitals remain stable by tomorrow morning, he'll be taken off the sedative drip and disconnected from the ventilator.

Sleep evades me that night.

I daydream about all the things we'll do once he wakes up. Ice skating, for instance, because, thanks to Madelyn, I've become quite good at it. And there's so much I want to tell him! But I know he won't simply open his eyes and be himself again right away. My concussion took time to recover from—how will he handle more than two weeks of deep sleep?

Restless, I retrieve the light blue sketchbook from my nightstand and leaf through it. Since my hospital discharge, I've added three new drawings. I avoided capturing the traumatic events, but I included a few moments from my return from Oregon. The instant I turned around in the horse stall to find him leaning against the door. A tender kiss in the hayloft. And the moment North asked if I wanted to spend the first night with him.

These memories are part of the beginning of our shared eternity, and I want to give them to North as soon as he's fully conscious.

Having abandoned sleep, I return the sketchbook to the drawer and, for the hundredth time in the past two weeks, open the WhatsApp chat history with North. I know each and every single word of this conversation, every period, every comma. They've etched themselves into my memory, just like North has into my heart. Sometimes, when I miss him too much, like now, I call his number. Of course, I know he won't answer. North's phone was destroyed in the accident. The experts found it in the wreckage, screen shattered. We salvaged the SIM card, but everything else was lost.

"The person you are trying to reach is currently unavailable."

I sigh, closing my eyes, cell phone still pressed to my

ear.

"Please try again at a later time."

The message is unchanging, even after the third call, but on this endless night, the comfort of these words feels better than nothing at all.

When the alarm finally goes off hours later, I bolt out of bed and get ready for work. I tackle my tasks at breakneck speed and devour my lunch just as fast, so we can head to the hospital as soon as possible. Ruth shares my excitement, as she's been on the same emotional rollercoaster these past few weeks, worrying and longing for her grandson.

Marie specifically arranged to be on duty today to be with us. She greets us with a radiant smile when we ring the bell outside the ICU. After sanitizing our hands, we follow her into North's room, and then I understand her elation.

North still lies motionless in his bed, reminiscent of Snow White after biting the apple, but the breathing machine is gone and his lips are relaxed and closed. My heart leaps within me.

Now, only a single IV is attached to his arm, and the bandage around his chest was removed two days ago. A thick vertical scar runs down the center of his ribs, but it has healed well, and the ward doctor said it would fade significantly in the coming weeks. Soon, it won't be so noticeable.

I've only managed to cope with North's absence by reminding myself that he doesn't experience the pain of healing like this. It's been a comforting thought for Ruth as well, but now she stands beside his bed, just as eager as I am, impatiently squeezing my fingers.

"How much longer until he wakes up?" I whisper to Marie. I don't even know why I'm speaking so softly. It's not like I want him to sleep forever. Over the past few days, I've shared countless stories by his bedside, while Ruth and I held his hands for hours. Yet, it's different knowing that he's no longer submerged in a dreamless darkness by medication and could open his eyes any moment if he hears our voices.

"We already reduced his medication at midnight and stopped it completely at six," Marie informs us, speaking a bit louder than I am. "So it shouldn't be much longer. Maybe another hour or two before he opens his eyes for the first time. He probably won't be fully awake until midnight, though, or perhaps not until tomorrow morning." She nudges me with her arm and grins. "You remember what it was like for you."

Yes. It was a nightmare. But I survived. And so will North...

Marie and I pull up two chairs so Ruth and I can sit beside North's bed while Marie returns to her duties. But first, she adjusts the head of the fully automated bed to make it easier for North to wake up.

And then we wait. Hour by hour.

But nothing happens.

Around five, my eyes start to droop, having not slept a wink the night before, but I force myself to stay awake. Rachel and Marie take Ruth out of the room for a bit to join them for coffee. The invitation is extended to me as well, but I don't want to leave. Visiting hours will be over at six, and until then, I'll continue to sit by his bed, waiting and hoping he finally awakens from his lengthy coma.

Without Ruth in the room for conversation, my head grows heavier, and I scoot the chair back, so I can lean against the wall and close my eyes for just a moment. I dream of ice-skating with North on a frozen lake. He curls his finger, beckoning me to join him. As I do, a subtle smile graces my lips, and I open my eyes.

North lies before me in bed, the monitor's steady heartbeat a comforting sound, and outside the large window, darkness envelops the world. But in that moment, the sun rises within me, and my heart leaps against the base of my throat. Because he has turned his head in the pillow towards me, and his beautiful dark blue eyes are open.

In an instant, my senses sharpen, and my first reflex is to jump up and rush to his side. But I remember all too well the confusion I felt after waking up from a coma, and I don't want to overwhelm North. I'm afraid that any sudden movement could shatter this miraculous moment, so I stay seated, swallowing tears of joy.

North blinks slowly, long intervals between each flutter. Bathed in the warm light above him and the blue glow of the monitors, he looks like an angel illuminated by the light of eternity.

My angel.

And *our* eternity.

I don't know if I've ever been as happy in my entire life as I am right now. Gently, I send him a small smile.

There's no change in his expression, but that's okay. I know he's still disoriented, and likely thirsty, too. When he'll get something to drink, however, is up to Marie.

Slowly, I stand and walk the short distance to his bed. His gaze follows me, captivated yet as tired as a newborn's. "Hey," I say, my voice barely audible as it falters. Then I tenderly reach for his hand. He accepts it, but offers no pressure in return. It doesn't matter. Soon, he'll regain his strength, and the North Star will shine brightly once more. "You can sleep now. I'm here."

For a few more seconds, he gazes silently, almost shyly, up at my face. Then his eyelids hesitantly lower halfway, and even though I can see his struggle to keep them open, they eventually close completely.

I wipe a tear of relief from my cheek and then gently run my fingers through his hair. "Good night, North..."

3. Forever is a place between yesterday and tomorrow

Releasing North's hand has never been harder than it was today. Ruth and I lingered by his bedside until Marie ushered us out, well beyond visiting hours. The petite nurse is working a 48-hour shift, so at least North will be in capable hands.

But sleep is elusive. I can't shake off the image of his shy, quiet gaze, as if he were trapped in a distant world where I'm a stranger. Tomorrow will be different, I reassure myself. And with that comforting thought, I finally drift into a realm of vivid dreams.

As I'd requested yesterday, Marie kept me updated on North's condition through WhatsApp. So when my alarm jolts me awake at five in the morning, three messages await me. North stirred briefly after midnight and was responsive by 2 AM. Half an hour ago, he managed to drink and keep it down. All fantastic news!

I shoot off a flurry of emojis and a "Catch you later!" before diving into my usual routine. But today, Ruth and I are too antsy to wait until after lunch for our hospital visit. I hop in the shower at eleven, and thirty minutes later, we're en route.

Anticipation has me buzzing, my mind racing with imagined first words. Maybe an "I've missed you!" or an "At last, you're back!" followed by a hug? With the inevitable crowd in the room, though, that may not be the best plan. Ruth hasn't found it strange that I've held North's hand daily for the past two weeks. I suspect it's because she sees me as another grandchild, and North has become like my brother in her eyes. For now, I want to preserve that image. We can let everything settle back into normalcy before deciding who to confide in about our budding romance.

My heart thumping, I press the buzzer outside the ICU and impatiently await Marie's usual arrival to fetch us. Surprisingly, it's Rachel who greets us, her freckled face devoid of the warm smile that typically graces her red curls.

"Hi, Adrian. Mrs. Beckett," she says, her tone almost formal, guiding us to the circular desk in the hallway where the nurse's station is situated. "Give me a moment. I'll let Marie know you're here."

Baffled, Ruth and I linger in front of the chest-high counter above the desk. I'm clueless about what's happening. But when I notice North's room door is closed—having been open since he arrived on this floor— a wave of nausea hits me. Cold sweat breaks out on my hands, and my breath grows unsteady.

Rachel raps gently on the glass door marked with a large number 2, then pokes her head through the slim opening. "His family's here now," we overhear her say in a hushed tone.

A chill races down my spine, and I sense Ruth growing uneasy beside me, her thoughts echoing my own nightmarish scenario.

At that moment, Marie emerges from room number two. Though she shuts the door behind her, I've already caught a glimpse of the room's emptiness. No bed in front of the monitors. Just a void.

As she nears us, I dash toward North's room. She intercepts me, her eyes swimming with concern that makes me want to scream. *Please, no!* Tenderly, she rests her hands on my forearms, holding me back.

I could easily lift her and clear a path, but what

would that accomplish? It wouldn't magically bring North back.

"What happened?" I stammer instead. "Where did they take him? I need to be with him!"

"Calm down, Adrian," Marie replies, a gravity in her voice I've never heard before. "Help me get your grandmother into the room." She gestures toward the room where I'd slept two weeks ago, already reaching for Ruth's arm. It's then that I notice I'm not the only one grappling with the situation. Ruth is ashen-faced, her aged eyes vacant.

Quickly, I assist. "I'm sorry, Ruth!" I mumble, realizing I'd been oblivious to her needs. We guide her into one of the red vinyl chairs, and I fetch her a glass of water.

"What happened to my grandson?" she mumbles, disoriented after taking a sip.

"I'm sorry, Mrs. Beckett, but this time you'll have to wait for the doctor to come," Marie says firmly, her gaze meeting mine. "He's on his way."

Just then, the electronic door outside opens, and I hesitantly step into the hallway. A doctor in a white coat approaches the station, flanked by two young nurses pushing a bed. And there lies North.

Oh my God, he's alive! Thank heavens!

Relief washes over me like a tidal wave, and I release a long, shaky breath.

Today, North dons a hospital gown. He's lost a bit of weight, but not enough to raise alarm. Despite looking exhausted, he listens to the doctor attentively. The brown-haired man spots me in the doorway and shoots a quick glance into our room. He places a reassuring hand on North's arm, telling him he'll be right back. The nurses push him past me—and he seems to entirely miss my presence.

What the—? Did he not see me just now?

Marie intercepts the doctor beside me and guides him to Ruth, introducing them. "Mrs. Beckett, this is Dr. Curtis. He'll explain what's happening with North now." The man, who radiates more of an artsy vibe than a seasoned doctor, gives her hand a brief squeeze before requesting Marie to close the door. Silently, she complies, ushering me out of the room with her.

"Hey," I protest. What gives? But she's already leading me to the circular counter above the desk.

"I'm sorry, Adrian, but this conversation is strictly for family members listed in the records. Dr. Curtis is adhering to protocol."

"Then tell me what's going on," I grumble softly, ensuring our conversation remains private. "I thought he was dead! But he's clearly okay. Where was he?"

"He had to go down for a CT scan because something with—"

"Marie, can you help me here, please?" Rachel's

voice interrupts from the nurses' station.

Marie sighs, clearly stressed, and briefly but firmly places her hand on my elbow. "Stay here! I'll be right back."

Where would I go? Stroll around the block?

The door of my former room is still closed, and I know I'm not supposed to barge in on Ruth and the doctor's conversation. Well, I won't. But I can still eavesdrop.

As Marie vanishes into the room behind the desk and the two nurses exit North's room shortly after, I find myself drawn elsewhere, though. Tentatively, I take a few steps toward room number two and peer inside from a distance. North lies still in his bed. The head of the mattress is raised halfway between upright and reclined, giving him a relaxed view of the entire room. And the door.

His eyes drift from the window to me as I hesitantly linger in the doorway. For a few seconds, he just stares at me. He looks good. Tired, but definitely grounded in reality again. I'm certain he knows where he is by now. And why. So why isn't he saying anything?

"Hi," I venture, trying to shatter the odd silence between us. "How are you?"

His throat bobs with a hard swallow before he parts his lips, wincing as if the words themselves are laced with pain. "It's all so damn exhausting." The intubation tube must have left its mark, but I want to cry tears of joy because it's the first sentence I've heard from him in weeks.

Resisting the urge to sprint over and envelop him in my arms, I approach his bed instead and reach for his hand. North, however, shyly pulls away, and a look into his eyes shatters my heart. I don't know what it means, but the sudden distance between us is palpable, like a thousand needle pricks on my skin.

"Are you—" His voice cracks before he tries again, hoarsely. "Are you part of my family?"

The question slams into me like a wrecking ball. "What?" I whisper, shaken.

"Rachel said my family was coming today." His tone is flat, devoid of emotion.

Inside, I feel the world come crashing down around me. "And you don't know who your family is—" The words scorch through me like molten lava.

Composed, North shakes his head, far more collected than I am. My lungs constrict, and my knees threaten to buckle.

My gaze drifts to the monitor displaying the rhythm of his heart. But it no longer beats for me. The steady beeping that once lulled me to sleep now grows deafening until I hear a voice screaming: *You've lost him!*

In a daze, my legs move sluggishly, as if wading through water. I brace myself on the foot of the bed and then the doorway to avoid collapsing. When the door to my old room opens, and Dr. Curtis escorts Ruth out, I know why she's crying. I know what he just told her.

Rachel appears from the nurses' station to tend to North's grandmother, but I just grab Marie's hand and pull her with me, continuing until we're out of the ward and into the chilly hospital corridor. "Adrian?" she asks, concern lacing her voice, but I can't answer her. Only when the door slides shut behind us do I release Marie, leaning on the wall with both hands. My head hangs between my outstretched arms, feeling like I'm about to retch onto my shoes.

"He doesn't remember me—" I choke out, breathless. Then I turn my head and lock onto her eyes, gripping the wall to stay upright. And I scream at her, "He doesn't know who I am!"

Marie's eyes glisten, as if she's fighting tears herself. She's holding up better than I am. "I know," she murmurs, rubbing my back gently. "Right now, he doesn't even know who *he* is. But falling apart won't help him, you hear me?" She pries my left hand from the wall and squeezes it reassuringly. "We're going to go back in there together now and wait for the CT results. And then we'll take it from there."

"I can't go back in there!" My voice is a desperate echo in the hallway. "What am I supposed to say to him?"

"You don't need to say anything. Just be there for

him, show him his family is ready to support him if he reaches out." She's well aware that I'm not actually part of his family, so why does she say that? Her gaze softens, and she whispers, "You both have already come so far. Giving up now isn't like you. We don't know the full story yet. Memory loss after an accident is common. With some luck, it could vanish just as quickly."

I know she's genuine. Empty encouragement isn't her style. That's how well I've gotten to know her over the past two weeks, and she seems to know me just as well.

When I take a deep breath and nod, she nods back, as if we've made a silent agreement. Then she releases my hand, walks with me through the door to the ICU, and together we enter North's room, where Ruth sits quietly crying by his bed, not holding his hand for once...

Though North greets me a second time with a small, discreet, almost curious smile, I remain near the door while Marie tends to his IV and adjusts things around his bed. The doctor reassures him and Ruth that his inflammation levels are normal to surprisingly good and that his post-operative recovery is going well. When asked about pain, North shakes his head. Then Rachel calls from the hallway, "Dr. Curtis? The CT results are in!" and the doctor steps out for a moment.

I'm desperate to know what North can still remember. If he's forgotten me, his grandma, and even himself—as Marie mentioned—does he recall anything from his life at all? Unwilling to make him speak and cause more pain, I stand silently by the wall, close to losing my mind, waiting for Dr. Curtis to return with a printed report in hand.

"The good news is—" he begins, addressing all of us with a sweep of his eyes. "The CT is normal. No aneurysm pressing on any areas of the brain."

A quiet sigh of relief escapes me. I couldn't handle another bombshell right now.

"But then what's causing his memory loss?" Ruth voices the question that weighs heavily on my heart, too.

"We believe it's post-traumatic amnesia, likely from the time of the accident."

As before, North swallows several times, his face twisted in pain, and then forces out the words, "How long until—"

"Until you remember everything again?" Dr. Curtis finishes for him. North nods, fear evident in his eyes. "Well, it's hard to say. Sometimes it takes just a few hours, a couple of days, or maybe even a few weeks—"

Since he leaves the sentence hanging, I mentally interject, feeling as drained as my phone battery at the end of the day, "But that's not always the case, right?"

Everyone's gaze shifts to me, and the doctor sighs as if he genuinely cares. Yet he maintains a professional distance from both North and the rest of us. "No, it's not. In some cases, memories never return." He turns back to

North, gently patting him on the shoulder. "But let's not assume that today. The likelihood of your memories being lost forever is extremely low compared to other outcomes."

The probability of a bear crossing the road right in front of a car is also incredibly low. And yet, it happened.

Oh my *God!* I hate myself for that thought. I should stay optimistic and not let today's events discourage me. North doesn't deserve that.

But it's becoming so damn hard...

When the doctor and the ICU nurses leave us alone with him, the room quickly falls into an awkward, suffocating silence that coils around us like a boa's grip. Ruth's fingers twitch repeatedly, as if she wants to reach for her grandson's hand, but something's holding her back. And I haven't moved an inch from the wall next to the door in the past forty-five minutes.

As North's eyes start to droop more frequently, I finally say in a calm and composed voice, "Ruth? We should leave now and let North rest. It's been a tough day for him." It's been tough for all of us.

"Of course," she stutters, rising from her chair. It's clear to all of us how difficult it is for her to leave her grandson alone in this bed. I'd feel the same way if I were closer to him. From here, it's easier to grit my teeth, put up an internal wall, and say goodbye for now. It doesn't mean that breathing has become any easier for me. Not in the slightest.

"Take care, North," I say softly, but only after I've turned my back on him. I don't wait for a response since I haven't even told him my name this afternoon.

In the hallway, the sad faces of Rachel and Marie greet us. "You're leaving already?" asks the red-haired nurse. She knows we usually stay much longer.

"North is tired. He needs to rest," I reply curtly. But before we can leave, we run into Dr. Curtis again, who has just returned to the ward.

"I'm glad you're still here," he says to both of us. "There are a few important things you should know about in this new situation. Can we sit down outside for a minute?"

We follow him out into the hospital corridor and lower into the line of blue vinyl chairs in the waiting area by the elevators.

"You need to understand that North's life started anew this morning," he says, mainly addressing Ruth since she's his closest relative. "His memory is like a blank hard drive that needs to be filled again. And you can't expect too much from him in the process."

I'm sure there are people in this world who would give anything to forget certain things from their past just like that. But I also know the wonderful memories North has lost. It's all so unfair!

"What do you mean by 'not expect too much'?" Ruth inquires.

"I know you want to help your grandson return to his old self as quickly as possible and reintegrate into your lives. But if you push too hard and too fast, it could backfire. Don't overwhelm him with too many people or situations from his old life at once. That can lead to mental and emotional overload, putting him under pressure."

Determined not to make any mistakes in the coming days, Ruth and I hang on his every word.

"Give him the space he needs to explore but don't push him. I understand North is studying at Calgary University?" Ruth nods, and the doctor continues, "He should take this semester off entirely and slowly find his way back home and into his environment before resuming his studies. Also, don't let too many friends reach out to him. You probably know your grandson best. Limit his contacts for now."

"Most of his friends are at the university. If he's not supposed to go there anymore, it won't be much of a problem," Ruth murmurs, clearly disheartened.

"Good. The same applies to a significant other," the doctor emphasizes, and I catch my breath. "If he's in a relationship, confronting him with it right now would be disastrous. The feelings he had for people in his life are currently foreign to him. To meet all those expectations, he might try to force himself to feel emotions that have no place in his mental recovery." He places his hand over Ruth's slightly trembling fingers in her lap. "Please ask your family members and his friends for patience. That's the only way they can truly help North at the moment."

She nods understandingly and assures him that North isn't in a relationship at the moment. She would know if he was.

Meanwhile, my world shatters for the second time today, and I wish this were all just a terrible nightmare from which I could finally awaken.

North doesn't remember us.

And I can't tell him what we used to be...

4. Snap out of it!

The next day, for the first time, I don't tag along with Ruth to visit North at the hospital. I've spent the entire night racking my brain about how to handle the situation. How to face North. What to say to him. How to act when our eyes lock.

But I'm no closer to answers. Because how do you fake indifference to someone who, in reality, means the world to you?

That's why I've chosen, for now, to keep my distance, regardless of the pain it brings. I don't want to corner him with emotions he may not reciprocate. And since he doesn't remember me, he likely won't care that I'm not there, silently sitting in a chair against the wall during visiting hours.

Thankfully, Dr. Valentine agrees to accompany Ruth. As North's assigned doctor, he has free access, and it's comforting knowing Ruth has someone who can support her grief more adeptly than I can.

I just wish someone could support me through mine.

Arriving back at the empty house after work, I stand behind the closed door for a moment, letting my gaze drift through the living room. The cozy tiled stove, the stairs, the kitchen entrance, and the couch with the quaint coffee table all remind me of North. His presence lingers, and I can almost hear him and feel his warmth when I close my eyes.

I attempt to preserve that warmth by taking a hot shower, but it's futile. With each passing moment, North feels further away, and no matter how hard I try, I can't hold on to him.

I step out of the shower, dry off, and slip into the T-shirt and jeans I brought. But as I try to return to my room, I stop in front of North's door. Since coming back from the hospital, I haven't entered his room once. It felt like an invasion of his privacy.

No, that's not entirely accurate. There was another reason.

With the door closed, I could delude myself into thinking he wasn't in the hospital but sitting behind the door, engrossed in a book. I could pretend he just needed some solitude and would join us downstairs soon.

But that illusion no longer holds.

Hesitantly, I lift my hand to the doorknob and turn it slowly. As the door creaks open, North's unique scent of Canadian forests and crisp winters washes over me, nearly bringing me to my knees. I take a long, deep breath, savoring the memories tied to that aroma. As I finally step into his cozy sanctuary, the low winter sun streams through the window, causing dust particles to dance in its golden light. Like ghosts of the past.

Approaching his desk, I gently run my fingertips along the edge. The list of all the fireflies remains on a stack of books, worn from frequent handling while I was in Oakspeak. And atop it all lie the black fingerless gloves with the white radioactive symbol.

When he wore them, they created an electrifying aura around him. Cool and enigmatic. Alluring. Like a secret I was dying to unravel from day one. Gently, I slip on the right glove and secure the narrow Velcro strap around my wrist. It fits perfectly. Putting on the left glove, I stretch my fingers out before me. The thought of how often he must have worn them, leaving those subtle signs of wear, warms me from within.

Draped over the back of the swivel chair is the black hoodie he wore the day I returned from Oakspeak. In white letters on the back, it reads: *Wicked Fireflies.* I pick it up and press it to my face. It's soft and warmed by the sunlight. When I close my eyes, it's as if he had just worn it. His scent still lingers, and my throat tightens.

With a pained sigh, I lower my hands and slowly spin in place. The bed is made, but there's a small indentation in his pillow, as if he'd collapsed onto the mattress for a moment before our trip to see Maddie that day. Probably while he was on the phone with her. I fixate on that spot for minutes, wishing he were still lying there, smiling at me like he always did.

Heavy-hearted, I shuffle across the floor and stop in front of his bed. Slipping my arms through the hoodie's sleeves, I zip it up and slowly sink onto the mattress. Feeling the weight of the world bearing down on me, I collapse sideways into his pillow, draw my legs onto the bed, and curl into a pathetic ball, hands clasped tightly under my chin.

For half an hour or more, I lie motionless where North usually rests, staring at the opposite wall. All the while, I wait for him to slide up behind me and wrap his arms around me, telling me everything's fine.

But he's not here. And when he returns, I won't have a place in this bed anymore.

The door, still half open, creaks further, and someone peeks around the corner. "Adrian?" Maddie asks, her voice laced with confusion. "Why are you at home and not with North at the hospital?"

Oh, I hadn't even considered her. When Ruth called her last night to share the sad news, they agreed Maddie would come over and clean after her shift at the grocery store today. Since she has her own key to the front door, it's no problem.

Unsure of what to say, I continue staring at the wall as she enters the room and releases such a poignant sigh that even the curtains seem to droop. "Oh my goodness. Of course..." Seeing me so forlorn, dressed in North's clothes, lying in his bed probably reveals a lot that she hasn't been able to glean from him. She quietly approaches the bed and sits cross-legged on the floor, directly in front of my face. Gently, she runs her delicate fingers through my hair. "You love him, don't you?"

I swallow hard and let my gaze meet hers, but I don't say anything.

"I wondered if he was the reason you cut your vacation short. I haven't seen him grin in a long time as much as he did that afternoon when you both visited me."

"Didn't he tell you anything?" I mumble into the pillow, hardly believing it given North's open nature, even though I appreciate that he apparently hasn't outed me to his best friend.

"Oh...he told me a lot," Maddie says softly, her voice intended to coax me out of my misery. But she doesn't succeed. "Mostly about how much it tormented him, not knowing whether you were rejecting his advances out of fear of the truth or because you genuinely didn't want anything to do with him. You put him through hell in the days leading up to Christmas, I can tell you that."

A fluttery sensation dances in my stomach at her words. "Really?" I ask, incredulous. I never pegged North for the insecure type.

"Totally. One night—I was working late at the store—he called me, frantic, because he needed these super specific bug stickers and couldn't find the right ones anywhere. They couldn't be bees or ladybugs, which are a dime a dozen. Nope, they had to be fireflies, like the world would end without them."

My eyes narrow, and a bittersweet smile tugs at my lips.

"I knew it had to be about you, but he wouldn't spill the details. When I sent him to the toy store and he finally found some, he was over the moon." Her fingers twirl a few strands of my hair, a comforting gesture that eases the ache of loneliness. "Guess you won't tell me why they had to be fireflies either, huh?"

I don't want to share that story today. But because she's managed to steer my thoughts in a slightly less gloomy direction, I fish my keychain out of my pocket and place it between us on the bed.

Madelyn's eyes widen with recognition. She grabs the metal firefly, its blue paint chipped in places. "This is North's Fireflies charm." Surprise washes over her face. "He's carried it for over two years, ever since he joined the team. That thing's sacred to him." Then she flips the nylon strap and sees the word written in his handwriting. "Forever..." she murmurs, looking at me in amazement. "So you two are—"

"We *were*," I correct her, my voice raw. "Now we're nothing, because he can't remember me. Or you. Or Ruth. He doesn't even remember his own name or what his life was like for the past twenty-one years."

"It's awful, I know. But it's not over, Adrian." She presses the keychain back into my hands. "You can help him remember."

"No, I can't," I croak, my gaze lost in the distance. "The doctor said confronting him with a relationship could overwhelm North. I can't tell him about us."

"Seriously? That's gonna stop you?" Maddie exclaims, tugging my hair to bring my focus back to her. "Get out of this bed, get dressed, and go see North at the hospital!"

"I don't want to." I'd rather hide here until everything's resolved and North comes back to me. Defeated, I slide the keychain into my pocket. "I can't even look him in the eyes without losing it. This is all so screwed up!"

"It is. But wallowing here because life threw a curveball won't help. So—snap out of it!"

"Easy for you to say. You didn't lose your first love in the accident."

"And neither did you! North's alive. He's awake.

And he's coming home soon. So what if he can't remember his time with you? Big whoop." Seeing my worried expression, she continues, "You wanna know something? The day he came home from college, before you even left the room, he was already asking me, starry-eyed, if I knew if you had a girlfriend. He fell in love with you once—he'll do it again! But definitely not if you're moping around here, sulking into his pillow."

Her vivid storytelling stirs a chuckle from me, but her candid pep talk also reignites a flicker of bravery.

"Do you really believe that?" I murmur.

"Yes...I'm absolutely certain." Her tone softens, as gentle as a whisper, and she does something that leaves me nearly speechless. She reaches under her sweater collar, pulls out a dark leather necklace, and leans down on the mattress, drawing her upper body close to mine. With warm fingers, she takes my left hand and closes it around the oddly shaped pendant. "Do you remember what this is, Adrian?" she asks, serene as the night sky.

Of course. "A shooting star..." It was a Christmas gift from me to her.

"That's right. I already used my wish for my mom. But you still have one left. So close your eyes and make a wish!"

Without hesitation, my eyelids fall shut, and deep in my heart, I envision North enveloping me in his embrace, smiling knowingly, and promising eternity for the two of us. My throat constricts, but a tiny spark of hope flickers within me. Shooting stars don't fall without reason, right? And a small miracle would be perfect right now.

As I release the meteorite fragment and Maddie tucks it back under her sweater, I offer her a soft but genuine "Thank you."

"No problem," she replies with a smile. "Now, come on!" Suddenly, she grabs my wrists, yanking me off the bed, and I land on my behind. I can only scuttle after her like a crab, as she doesn't release me until we reach the door. "If you won't go to the hospital, at least help me clean up the house."

I leave the cleaning to her. But in exchange, I make us hot chocolate in the kitchen, which we savor together in the living room by the fireplace. When Ruth comes home later and joins us with a cup of herbal tea, she shares how well North is handling the complex situation, and how much she had to tell him about his childhood and youth in response to his questions. As she speaks, her smile outshines her tears, casting a shimmer of hope over all of us. "Also, the doctor said his circulation is remarkably stable after waking up, and he can come home soon if everything continues going well," she announces joyfully.

And that joy steadily grows within me, too.

*

Although I wake up on Thursday with the resolve to either seize fate by the horns or kick it in the rear, following Maddie's advice, Ruth goes to the hospital alone to visit North that afternoon. Symphony, the white mare, has injured her leg in the paddock, and we had to call the veterinarian. Since his arrival time was uncertain, someone had to stay home. I volunteered, unwilling to steal Ruth's precious time with her grandson.

Thankfully, Symphony's injury is minor, just a muscle strain in her left hind leg. The elderly veterinarian, clad in blue overalls and familiar with the mare since her foal days at another farm, leaves me an ointment to apply twice daily for the next few weeks. I can manage that.

After I've settled all the horses in their stalls in the late afternoon and am climbing the stairs to my room, my phone buzzes in my pocket. I pull it out to read the message. It's from Marie, and it actually coaxes a small smile from me.

Marie

North asked about you today.

I know that doesn't mean he remembers me, but at least I crossed his mind today. A tiny spark of hope flutters within me.

Alright, then. Tomorrow, I'll move heaven and earth to visit him in the ICU again.

My pulse quickens as I stroll alongside Ruth, crossing the short distance from the automatic doors to the room marked with a frosted glass "2." Today, the usual cacophony of beeping monitors is absent. I can already see North propped up in his bed, engaged in lively conversation with a blonde nurse I've only seen on a couple of our visits. Joanna, the nurse I recognize, raps gently on the door. "You've got company," she tells North with a warm smile before slipping out of the room with her colleague.

I let Ruth enter first, and like our last visit, I linger by the door instead of approaching North's bedside. I don't want my nerves to betray me through my unsteady breaths. Yet, my heart skips a beat when North looks my way and offers a guarded, "Hi."

"Hey... You're looking good," I respond. He truly does, especially compared to his frail state over the past few weeks. I cling to that observation. Everything else...will improve. "You don't sound as rough as you did a couple of days ago."

He rubs his throat and manages a wry grin. "Yeah, they finally stopped feeding me nails. Now there's pudding for dessert."

Despite losing so much in the accident, North's sense of humor apparently remained unscathed. His quip eases my anxiety, calming me in more ways than just one.

That afternoon, I watch in amazement as North peppers Ruth with questions, as if his mind is an empty book, eager to be filled by the weekend. It's heartwarming to see his cheerfulness unmarred.

When Ruth steps out for a moment to use the restroom and fetch a glass of juice from the kitchenette, North gestures to the second chair near his bed. "You wanna sit?"

Truthfully, I don't. I've been leaning against the wall, maintaining a safe distance to keep my emotions in check. But I yield to his request. I grab the backrest of the chair and swivel it around, straddling it. This way, it's less apparent that I'm still sitting a good distance from his bed. I casually rest my arms on the green backrest, noting that each room in this ward seems to have its own distinct color scheme.

"Can I ask you something?" North inquires, adjusting his legs under the blanket.

My shoulders lift in a nonchalant shrug. "Sure. Anything."

"What are we to each other?"

Anything but *that.*

I open my mouth, but words escape me. North quickly picks up the conversation, as if realizing he's put me in an uncomfortable position and wants to smooth things over. "I haven't quite pieced it together from

Grandma's stories. And most of it is still pretty confusing, especially when she gets carried away and her thoughts bounce around like a pinball."

I've witnessed firsthand how animated the old lady can become when she reminisces about the past. But the fact that North calls her *Grandma* instead of *Grams*, like he used to, fills me with an unsettling sadness.

"She talks about you as if we're brothers," he attempts to clarify, his face contorted in a puzzled expression. "But yesterday, she told me I'm an only child. And my father was supposedly her only son. I can't quite put the pieces together. Are you adopted?"

Oh Jeez, I can't help but laugh. "No, I wasn't adopted. But then, in a way, I was."

"I don't get it."

I can't blame him for being confused, but it feels good to find humor in this messed-up situation for once. "I'm from Oakspeak, Oregon."

"The States?"

"Exactly." Thankfully, not all of his geographic memory has been erased. "That's where my family lives. You guys hired me for the winter because your grandmother needed help with the horses while you're away at college."

"We have horses?"

"Yes. Didn't Ruth tell you?"

"No. I thought we had a dog?"

Oh boy. She must not have delved too deep into his life story yet. "You used to have one. That was ages ago. Now it's just you, her, six horses in the stable, and a tomcat in the hayloft."

"Ah, I see." He furrows his brow, and I can almost hear his brain working overtime. "And what about you?"

"I've only been at the farm for about two months."

"So we're not related?" His tone conveys neither disappointment nor happiness—only sheer bewilderment that tugs at my heart.

I shake my head.

"Then we're...friends?"

It takes a moment for me to steady my voice. "Yes, we are. Very good friends, actually."

"And Grandma loves you because—"

"Because your grandmother is the most compassionate woman in the world and genuinely cares for everyone around her," I tell him earnestly.

"Yeah..." North murmurs, his gaze drifting towards the door. "I've noticed she's an incredibly lovable person. It's easy for me to see her as family." His throat bobs as he swallows hard. "But I'm still scared to leave this room in a few days and move into her house." Slowly, he turns his head back to me. "Can you believe that?"

His apprehensive words send a chill down my spine. I hadn't considered his point of view. It must be terrifying for him. Since he woke up, this room and hospital are all he knows. The farm where he grew up is now an entirely new world. Everything there is unfamiliar, including the people.

"I get what you're feeling," I offer him some reassurance. "But it's also your home. I bet you'll adjust in no time. We'll all be there to help you. And if it's really that daunting, just think of it as a brief farm getaway. No pressure, no obligations. Just a relaxed time to rediscover the world."

He ponders my suggestion for a moment. And at the end of his reflection, a smile breaks through. "You're right. It doesn't seem so bad when I look at it that way."

I'm relieved to see the spark of confidence return to his eyes.

The next minute, Ruth comes back with her juice from the kitchenette and settles into the chair on the other side of the bed. For a while, I stay put, captivated by the elderly woman's elaborate tales full of time leaps. But after about fifteen minutes, I feel the need for distance, realizing I'm getting lost in North's mesmerizing eyes, which isn't ideal. I stand with my back to him at the window and quietly sigh, watching the sun dip behind the snow-capped forests to the west. What will the new morning bring?

When it's time to leave, Ruth tenderly clasps her grandson's hand for the first time, squeezing it with all the love she can muster. I then offer my distant goodbye and follow Ruth out of the room.

"Hey, Adrian?" North's tentative voice calls after me, and I turn to face him. "Can I ask you something else?"

I nod, tell Ruth I'll catch up, and stand in the doorway to Room Two.

"You were here a few days ago when I first woke up, right?" He cocks his head, his eyes clouded with confusion, as if his memory is playing tricks on him again. "I didn't imagine that. Did I...?"

A warmth envelops me, like a gentle spring breeze following a harsh winter. "No. You didn't imagine it," I reply, my smile more heartfelt than visible. "See you soon, North."

As I turn and trail after Ruth to the exit, I hear his soft words behind me, "Good night, Adrian."

And they mean the world to me.

5. The thin line between love and distance

North has been holed up in his room for hours. Ruth brought him home from the hospital this morning while I was busy with the horses. He's made remarkable progress in the past five days, and the doctors were confident he could continue healing on his own from this point on.

From the stable, I watched the pickup truck roll into the driveway, and both of them stepped out. Every fiber of my being wanted to drop the pitchfork and race to meet them. But North looked so lost and vulnerable that I didn't want to smother him with a grand welcome. And when Ruth took his hand and guided him into the house, I knew he was in good hands.

Now, I'm sitting in the spacious armchair in the living room, struggling to concentrate on the sketchpad resting in my lap. I keep stealing glances at the staircase, second-guessing my decision. North didn't join us for lunch, even though Ruth prepared his favorite dish—pork tenderloin in a savory wine sauce. She even whipped up a cherry pie for dessert. The mouthwatering aroma fills the house, potent enough to lure wolves from the forest. But neither the scent nor Ruth's thoughtful gesture seem to reach North.

When Dr. George Valentine drops by in the late afternoon to check on North and catch up as his trusted physician, Ruth sends him upstairs, as he's familiar with the house. I hear his gentle knock on the door above, then toss my drawing supplies on the table, get dressed, and head out to the paddock. I need a breath of fresh air. The endless anticipation of North finally emerging from his room is driving me up the wall.

Brushing snow off the fence's crossbar, I lean on it with my arms folded, watching the horses huddle together for warmth at the sheltered feeding station. They press close in the chilly air, while I stand out here, isolated. Sometimes, it's tough not to curse the universe for stealing away my *forever* with North.

"Hello, Adrian," the familiar, gravelly voice of Dr. Valentine greets me after about half an hour, and as I turn my head over my shoulder, he comes to stand beside me.

"How is he?" I blurt out immediately, feeling like George Alexander Valentine is my only lifeline to North today.

"He's doing well. The new situation is still a bit daunting for him, but he's already started exploring his own room. That's a good sign; his curiosity will help him adjust to his surroundings before long." He pauses for a moment, then squeezes my shoulder reassuringly. "But how are you?"

I'm puzzled by his question.

"Right now, it seems like the whole world revolves around North. We shouldn't forget that you were in the car, too. You've been through a lot yourself."

"I'm fine," I dismiss quickly, as I'm not the one who needs looking after here. The pain from my bruises has almost vanished, and I only felt dizzy for the first few days in the hospital.

"Are you sure?"

Uncertain of what he's getting at, I narrow my eyes.

"Ruth mentioned that you haven't quite shaken off the accident. She says that every time you pass the spot in the woods where it happened, you close your eyes and start to sweat a little."

She noticed that? Oh boy.

A shrug rolls off my shoulders. "It's not that bad. It'll get better." It's nowhere near as bad as the first time we passed the spot or when I saw the car wreck in the workshop's backyard. "Time is a great healer..." or so they say.

"Yes, it is," Dr. Valentine replies as softly as his voice allows. And because he seems to sense that I don't have much more to say on the subject, his gaze drifts off into the distance. But his words linger within me.

"Can I ask you something personal?" I murmur after a quiet minute, waiting for him to turn his head back towards me.

"Of course."

I clear my throat quietly. "What happened between you and Ruth that made her so angry with you for such a long time? She only mentioned you once, but it sounded like something really terrible had occurred."

The doctor, who can't seem to bring himself to retire and leave his small community, lets out a wistful sigh. "It happened a long time ago," he begins to share his story. "When I met Ruth Beckett, she was already a widow. I fell in love with her right away, but she was still mourning her Edric too deeply to be open to new love. Regardless, I didn't give up, and after a long time, she finally gave us both a chance." A smile appears in his old eyes. "I was the happiest man in the world."

I think I know that feeling.

But the expression vanishes from his face almost immediately, and his features become somber and sad. "Our happiness didn't last long. Her son had an accident on the farm."

He fell off the barn roof, I know. Sylvia Brunswick told me.

"His death sent Ruth spiraling into a deep depression. And when North's mother Emily died of severe pneumonia the following year, Ruth blamed me for not being able to save her as a doctor. We tried everything, but in the end, the medications just couldn't help her anymore."

That's a heart-wrenching story. I don't know who I feel more sympathy for among all those involved. Ruth Beckett's life is littered with far too many tragedies. And now, there's the situation with North as well.

"The fact that you saved her grandson's life must have made up for a lot," I deduce.

"I wish that hadn't been the reason, but yes, you're right. And I'm glad she's letting me back into her life now." He turns around and looks both concerned and hopeful toward the farmhouse, from where warm light spills through the windows onto the snow. "You know," he continues, "no other woman has touched my heart after Ruthie. But sometimes, life does offer you a second chance."

I hope so...

The words die in his mouth, and he straightens, clearing his throat as if to end our journey into the past. He gives me one more reassuring pat on the shoulder.

"Gotta go, lad, another patient's waiting. I'll be back tomorrow to check on all of you."

"See you, Dr. Valentine," I reply with a nod.

Once he's gone, I bring the horses in from the paddock and head back to the inviting warmth of the living room. A single glance at Ruth in her rocking chair tells me North is still hiding away in his sanctuary. I won't let it discourage me, though. He needs time to explore and process, and I'll give him that. I wrap the cozy blanket Ruth gifted me after Christmas around my shoulders and sink into the armchair, working on my drawing. It's coming along, providing a welcome distraction until North finally emerges.

It's not until after nightfall that he makes an appearance, and if it wasn't for the faint movement in the corner of my eye, I might not have noticed him at all. Surprised but silent, I turn to see him hesitating on the landing, gripping the railing. He looks so out of place that it sends a shiver down my spine. Uncharacteristically, he's sporting faded jeans and a vibrant red sweatshirt. The contrast to his typical monochrome attire is jarring, but I have to admit, it suits him.

Without speaking, I lift my eyebrows and press my lips together, acknowledging him. Then, with a slight nod toward the couch, I invite him to join us. He tentatively accepts, but as soon as Ruth hears him, she springs from her rocking chair to welcome him at the foot of the stairs.

"Hello, darling! How are you feeling?" she asks, her voice trembling with excitement and anxiety. "Do you want to eat something? I could warm up some lunch leftovers."

"Thanks..." he mumbles, self-consciously ruffling his ash and caramel hair. "But I'm not really hungry."

"Are you sure? You haven't eaten all day. Or maybe you'd like some cherry pie? It's fresh. You used to love it."

My heart aches for them both as Ruth tries so hard and North struggles with his confusion. He can't remember what he used to like, but the weight of his grandmother's hope bears down on him.

"Ruth, it's okay!" I interject, setting my drawing supplies on the table and heading to them, so I can loop an arm around Ruth to guide her back to her rocking chair. She should continue knitting and let her grandson breathe. "We can make a sandwich later if he gets hungry."

"Oh, heavens! Yes, of course—" she blurts out, realizing her overenthusiasm nearly smothered him. Picking up her knitting needles with a sigh, she refocuses on the dark pink wool hat she's been making for Maddie.

Meanwhile, North sends me a covert, grateful glance and forms the silent words, "Thank you." I respond with a smile and return to my seat, giving him space. The fact that he sits down across from me sends a thrill through my core.

"What are you drawing?" he inquires after a moment.

I hold up the paper and angle it for him to see.

"Wow!" he exclaims, genuinely impressed. "Is that Marie?"

"Mm-hm." I rest the portrait of our ICU nurse on my lap again and refine the shimmering aura that surrounds her flowing gown. In her hand, she holds a magic wand with a star at its tip, and tiny hummingbirds flutter around the hoops in her ears. On her bare upper arm, I've sketched a delicate silver bracelet adorned with gemstones that sparkle as much as her eyes.

Unexpectedly, North stands up and comes around the coffee table to join me. He leans over the back of my chair to inspect my artwork. "Wow, that's incredible," he murmurs close to my face. "It's like a fairy tale."

Obviously, North had showered earlier and used his old shower gel. The scent fills my nostrils and taunts me for not being able to do anything but sit here and grit my teeth. How I'd love to turn to him in this moment and tell him all the things I've been holding back for days. Things like: *I miss you.* And: *Do you remember…?*

Instead, I force a neutral "thank you" through my teeth and try to focus all my attention on the person in front of me rather than the one beside me.

"Adrian is quite the artist," Ruth cautiously adds from near the fireplace. "He's drawn all of us at some point."

As I see in the corner of my eye that North tilts his head toward me, I also turn to face him. Of course, I shouldn't, but it's an irresistible reflex. And then there are only his beautiful deep blue eyes, reminiscent of the sky before sunrise. Before a new morning. Before the return of a special memory...

But it doesn't come back. Instead, a question is now clearly written in his gaze.

Me, too?

Yes, you too, North.

"It's just a hobby. Nothing special," I deflect, taking the opportunity to free myself from his captivating gaze.

With that, North straightens up and takes a few steps toward the kitchen, but then hesitates. "May I—" He turns back to us and starts again. "Could I maybe have something to drink?"

Swinging my legs over the edge of the chair, I stand up to lead him to the kitchen. As I open the refrigerator and hold it invitingly up for him, I firmly tell him, "You live here, North, and aren't a guest. You don't have to ask if you want something. Everything in this house belongs to you, too."

"I know," he murmurs softly, so full of pain that it clenches my stomach. "But it's all so strange." And then he lifts his lost gaze back to my eyes. "Don't you think?"

My hand grips the refrigerator door handle so tightly

that my knuckles turn white. "You have no idea how…" I mutter almost inaudibly and then leave him alone in the kitchen.

I need to be more cautious here. As much as I crave his closeness, it constantly tempts me to do things that are simply too risky. I haven't touched him since that evening when he first opened his eyes again. And I miss it terribly.

As I put the finishing touches on the drawing, North returns to the living room with a small bottle of mineral water. He stands in front of the tiled stove, warming his back. Ruth takes the opportunity to explain that tomorrow morning, a representative from the agency that insured his black Ford Ranger will drop by to sort out a few things. Basically, North only has to sign some papers, and the insurance payout for the total loss will be transferred to his account.

"I wonder if I can even drive a car anymore?" he muses aloud.

That's an intriguing question.

"Let's find out!" I spontaneously suggest, surprising even myself.

"What do you mean?"

"Well…" I shrug and give a lopsided grin. "There's a pickup outside."

It takes mere seconds for an adventurous spark to ignite in his eyes. Yes, that's the guy I know! I slip the drawing into my leather portfolio and zip it up.

Unfortunately, Ruth's concern is palpable as she sets her knitting needles in her lap. "Do you really think that's a good idea, Adrian?"

"Why not? There's no traffic on the road up here at this time, and he's not alone." Seeing the worry lines deepen around her eyes, I immediately understand her real concern. The last time we got into a car together, we almost didn't make it out alive. "Nothing will happen to us," I assure her with a bit more seriousness and confidence in my voice. "So...may we borrow your car for a little practice drive?"

"Pleeeease..." North adds, so skillfully as if he suddenly remembers exactly how to persuade his Grams to get what he wants. Ruth and I both stare at him in shock for a moment, the silence so intense that you could almost hear our racing heartbeats. The shock passes quickly, though, as we realize we've let our hopes get carried away. North doesn't remember any of it. It's just his character that occasionally emerges from the black hole where his memories are hiding.

But that doesn't matter. And actually, it's wonderful. Because even without his memory, he's slowly becoming the person he once was. And the one I fell in love with.

"All right," Ruth finally relents with a smile. "The key is on the board."

North and I get dressed, and I can't tell who's more excited in this moment, him or me? From the board by the door, I grab Ruth's key ring with the reindeer charm and, as we walk down the porch to the red pickup, I toss the jingling keys to North in a small arc. "You drive."

His face lights up like a child's as he slides behind the wheel and pulls the seatbelt across his chest. Seemingly, he no longer feels any pain in that area after the surgery.

"Insert the key and turn it," I instruct him as I fasten my own seatbelt.

He manages to coax the old rust bucket into life until the engine hums contentedly under the hood. So far, so good. And just as a precaution, I explain to him, "Press the clutch, shift gears, and—"

At that moment, North already pivots to look behind him, placing a hand on my seatback, and reverses the car so swiftly out of the driveway that the tires spin on the snow-covered ground. We slide in a precise 180-degree spin, coming to a stop with the nose facing the road.

"Whoa!" I exclaim, eyes wide as I stare through the windshield. Then I turn to North, meeting his mischievous grin.

"Guess that still works," he says playfully, waggling his eyebrows so wickedly that a tingling shiver runs down my spine.

"Seems like it," I reply with a laugh.

"Shall we take a little spin?"

The twinkle in his eyes is downright intoxicating.

"Take a right up ahead," I direct him, because even though he seems to have mastered every maneuver behind the wheel, he's definitely lost in this part of town. Thankfully, he eases off the gas as we cruise past the Harris Farm and veer west towards the heart of Moonbreak Falls. We circle the town before merging onto the forest road that leads home.

And then out of nowhere, my heart starts to pound. I thought I had tamed the beast within, but I never considered how different it would be driving this path with North, instead of his grandma. The snow-laden fir trees on either side of the road resemble a work of art, as if Christmas elves had dusted them with icing sugar, conjuring up an enchanted winter wonderland. But beneath the illusion lies a deadly truth. We're still a good 500 meters from that fateful spot, but I'm already gasping for air. Sweat clings to my skin beneath my clothes.

I gulp and switch off the car's heater, my throat parched and aching. That's when North's gaze meets mine for the first time, worry creasing his brow. "You okay?"

"Yeah," I reply tersely, unzipping my jacket beneath the seatbelt before cracking the window open. An icy breeze fills the cab.

"Doesn't look like it."

"I'm fine. Just a bit warm in here."

North raises an eyebrow at my comment. "At minus fifteen degrees?" But I can't help it; I need the fresh air.

As we approach the spot where the bear materialized from the darkness, I sink deeper into my seat. North's eyes dart between me and the windshield, piecing together the puzzle. "Did it happen here?" he asks, his voice soft and understanding.

Eyes clenched shut, I grip my jeans tightly. "Just ahead, after the bend."

Without even looking, I can feel the car slowing to a stop. North pulls over and cuts the engine. What is he doing? I pry my eyes open, my breathing heavy. The pickup's headlights illuminate the exact spot where North had lain in the snow, revived by paramedics. The scene has been buried under fresh snowfall, leaving nothing visible except a broken snow pole leaning against a tree.

Why hasn't anyone cleaned it up, for Christ's sake?

When the driver's side door creaks open, I startle. North slips out and slams the door shut. I watch him, transfixed, as he takes a few steps in the harsh light. My heart feels as if it's frozen in place, not even a single beat.

I never imagined I'd get out of the car here again. But, against all odds, I reach for the door handle and push the heavy, old door open.

As the creaking sound echoes through the forest, North glances back at me. In that moment, I envy his amnesia of that harrowing night. How I wish I could scrub that memory from my brain. But it's there, suffocating me under an avalanche of panic and pain.

As I take another step, there's a crunch beneath my shoe. My gaze drifts downward, and I sweep away a dusting of snow with my toes. Glass. *Oh, God!* Glass! From North's SUV—the side windows, the windshield—all shattered.

All of a sudden, I'm transported back to that disastrous night amid the raging snowstorm. The black Ford is flipped on its roof, headlights casting beams into the void. And somewhere in the chaos, paramedics fight for North's life.

"Still no pulse!"

Voices from the past surge through my memory, and I double over, my hands bracing against my knees. The sound of my own breathing intensifies, as if the memories are forcing my head underwater while the night pulses with a haunting blue glow.

"Adrian?" A single, distant voice emerges, one that doesn't belong in this chaotic scene. It's just an echo, indiscernible amidst the turmoil. I can't find my bearings; there's too much happening around me. Perhaps the voice wasn't real—maybe I just wished for it.

It had vanished for far too long. Countless days and nights...

"Adrian—" the voice slices through my shattered world again, closer now. "Come on, look at me!"

I can't. I'm choking.

"Breathe. With me."

Strong hands grasp my shoulders, then cradle my neck beneath my jaw. Gently, they tilt my head up to meet a pair of warm, dark eyes. North crouches before me, one knee in the snow, and with his deliberate deep breaths, he guides me back to a rhythm that keeps me from passing out.

He allows me half a minute to regain control, all the while inhaling and exhaling the crisp winter air with me. "That's good," he says soothingly, helping me to my feet. Without the support of my knees, my hands instinctively search for something to cling to. North lets my fingers dig into his thick jacket, his gaze never wavering.

My breath still comes in gasps, and I'm unsure how long my legs will support me. Then, he pulls me close and gently wraps his arms around me. At first, I can't comprehend his actions, but in the next instant, I close my eyes and press my face against his shoulder. I understand that, for North, it's merely a caring gesture. But for me, right now, it's so much more.

Battling the tempest of emotions within me, I fight back tears, refusing to let them breach the surface.

And then he murmurs into my ear, "I'm so sorry, Adrian."

I know what he's apologizing for, even if he doesn't remember it. The world whirls around me, my throat tightening as I force the words from my chest, "It wasn't your fault."

Only the stars can tell how long we stand there on the forest roadside. Perhaps it's just ten seconds. Maybe it's an entire hour. But this time with North heals something deep inside me.

My hands and feet are ice-cold as we finally drive home that night, my knees stiff from the ordeal. None of us utters a single word for the entire ride.

We arrive just as Ruth heads upstairs to bed. She bids us goodnight, and I wait until she's vanished around the corner before collapsing onto the couch, an arm draped over my eyes. My feet hover awkwardly, half in the air and half on the ground, as I haven't managed to remove my shoes yet. My jacket lies discarded beside the coat hooks.

For a moment, I lie still, the crackling fire in the stove painting a peaceful scene, until North's voice interrupts the tranquility. "Need a hand getting undressed?"

I peek from beneath my arm, finding him perched on the coffee table, water bottle in hand— the one he'd grabbed from the fridge before our wild escapade. As I sit up, he hands it to me.

With trembling fingers, I unscrew the cap and gulp down a generous mouthful.

"That was some crazy-ass stunt you pulled," he says softly, a hint of accusation in his tone. "I honestly thought you were gonna drop dead."

"Thanks," I retort, sarcasm dripping from my words. "Right back at ya." And I don't just mean tonight. He must know that.

"Feeling better now?"

I take another swig before sealing the bottle and nod, leaning back against the plush cushion. What a wild ride it's been.

As North lingers on the low table before me, an eerie silence fills the room, as heavy as Ruth's wool blanket. After a beat, I break the quiet, asking, "Does it still hurt?" I deliberately touch my chest, making sure he understands my meaning.

"You mean the scar?"

I nod. "And everything beneath it."

He shakes his head. "It was a bit weird the first few days after I woke up. But now, I hardly feel a thing." In a sudden, swift gesture, he lifts his red sweatshirt and the white T-shirt beneath, revealing his torso. "Looks pretty good already, huh?"

The cut has indeed healed well. But the sight, so intimate and unexpected, leaves me breathless. I set the bottle on the couch beside me and inch forward. As if possessed, my hand reaches up, fingertips brushing tenderly over the slender scar bisecting his chest. His body is as warm as I remember from that one shared night in his bed, when his skin was still smooth and perfect. I recall how his skin smelled as I laid my head on that very spot, listening to his steady heartbeat for what felt like an eternity.

As North tugs his sweatshirt back down, brushing my hand away, my gaze snaps to his puzzled expression. Horrified at my boldness, I swallow hard and manage to croak out a thoroughly inappropriate, "I'm sorry."

He hesitates for a second before rising wordlessly and heading upstairs. My heart drums a rebellious beat in my chest, but I can't stop him. Defeated, I sink back into the cushion, burying my face in my hands, and groan silently into my fingers.

Damn it! What the hell was I thinking?

6. Obscure experiments

The moment I regain my composure, I spring up from the couch, kick off the boots I'd haphazardly thrown on for the ride with North in the truck, and toss a few logs into the stove to warm up the room. Then I head upstairs to my humble sanctuary. At my desk, I pull out Marie's drawing and study it under the soft glow of the lamp. I'm proud of my work. Maybe I'll surprise her with it at the hospital one day as a small token of gratitude for being my unexpected fairy godmother.

After adding it to the growing collection of drawings on the table, I collapse onto my bed. There, I retrieve the light blue sketchbook from the nightstand drawer, realizing that North won't get his hands on it anytime soon. It doesn't matter. I've decided to fill its pages with all the significant moments we share, though we're apart. That includes the accident, our time in the hospital with the steady rhythm of heartbeats on the monitors, and our tender embrace in the woods tonight.

When I began sketching in this book around Christmas, I'd envisioned a heartwarming, uplifting narrative. But it seems there's no fairy tale without its fair share of twists and turns. Perhaps it's those very challenges that make a series of events a genuine story.

I'm absorbed in adding shading to accentuate North's muscles on his bare, scar-branded torso when an unexpected knock on my door interrupts my concentration. "Come in!" I call out softly, hastily shutting the book in my lap as North steps inside.

"Hey, do you know—WHOA!" His eyes widen in astonishment, taking in the room and momentarily forgetting his question. "What's up with this place? Am I the golden child, and you're Cinderella?"

I can't help but chuckle at his observation. His room is a luxurious haven compared to mine. "I told you before, you live here. I'm just the help, and this is the guest room." But honestly, it doesn't bother me. It may be less than half the size of North's bedroom and furnished more modestly, but it's cozy and radiates an unmatched warmth.

Curiosity piqued, North strides over to my desk. There aren't many intriguing things to find here, but the scattered drawings seem to captivate him.

"What was it you wanted to ask?" I prod, but I can already tell from his posture and focus on the papers that he's only half-listening.

"My computer is password-protected," he mumbles, lost in thought. "Do you have any clue what password I need to use?"

Even if I were to suggest *SatanIsMyMaster666* right now, it'd barely register with him. So I keep quiet for the time being and slip the light blue book back into the drawer.

"Grandma was right. You're seriously talented," he says then with sincere admiration in his voice. "They're incredible." Thumbing through them all, one by one, he suddenly falls silent. For a long moment, he stands still, his gaze locked on a single drawing. I know exactly which one. The Angel Warrior. But the thoughts it provokes in him remain concealed.

At last, he gathers the papers into a neat stack and glances around. The black fingerless gloves adorned with the radioactive symbol catch his eye. He picks them up, remarking, "Cool gloves you've got here."

"Actually, they're yours," I admit, remembering that I'd left them here a few days ago after trying them on in North's room along with the hoodie.

"Oh," he says, surprised.

The hoodie itself still drapes over the back of my desk chair. Naturally, he notices it, too, and reads the lettering on the back.

"Grandma told me I play college ice hockey, and I found two jerseys with this name in my closet," he states, looking baffled. "Are we teammates or something?"

"No," I mumble, feeling trapped by the situation. "That's both yours."

He cocks his head towards me and silently arches an eyebrow before a hint of suspicion laces his voice. "There's quite a bunch of my stuff in your room."

Shoot, yes!

I maintain a poker face and meet his gaze. Then I shrug it off. "You've been in here a few times."

Doubt flashes in his eyes before he drawls, "Okay..." in a tone that suggests it's far from okay, and I've just handed him a mystery needing more clues. But he seems to accept I won't provide them tonight.

North leans against my desk, his butt resting on the edge, and grips the sides. "Got plans for tomorrow?" he switches gears, and I'm relieved.

Still, his question awakens something within me, and the butterflies in my stomach, which have been fluttering more frequently when he's near. "I work at the stable every morning," I tell him.

"And in the afternoon?"

"What do you have in mind?" I counter.

"On my desk, there's a busted phone. I wanna buy a new one and check what's on my SIM card. Maybe there're some photos that'll jog my memory."

Initially, I panic because he shouldn't read our WhatsApp messages. Then again, the app is usually tied to the device, not the number. So his chat history should have been wiped with his old phone. No need to freak out.

"I could use a tour guide," he adds with hope in his eyes. "But I don't wanna impose on Grandma."

Shopping with Granny isn't hip, huh? The thought makes me grin, and I nod. "No worries. I'd be happy to show you around. We can head out after lunch."

As if on cue, his stomach rumbles like a bear hibernating inside, and he looks sheepish. "Is that sandwich offer still good?"

Chuckling, I get up from the bed. "Absolutely. Let's go."

We tiptoe down the stairs, careful not to disturb Ruth, and only flick on the light when we're in the kitchen. I take a seat at the table to give him space, but North stands bewildered before me, gripping the back of a chair as if he's throttling it. Adjusting will likely take him some time.

I hop off the chair and head to the fridge. "How about roast beef and salad?" I ask, pulling out a few other items.

"Sounds good." North leans against the kitchen counter, watching as I neatly arrange the ingredients on a slice of bread. At the last moment, I spread some peanut butter on top. "You sure that belongs in there?" he asks, dubious.

"I'm the one making it, so I choose what goes in." It's that simple. Plus, I'm curious to see if he still hates peanut butter like he used to without his memories. Maybe...

I fold the sandwich, slice it diagonally, hand him one half, and keep the other on the plate. Then I hoist myself onto the kitchen counter, letting my legs dangle, and take a big bite.

North remains wary of my creation, examining it from all angles.

"Just try it!" I urge him, as I've almost polished off my half.

He nibbles cautiously at a corner, letting his eyes wander while obviously testing the flavor on his tongue. Interesting. This time he doesn't spit it out. And it doesn't seem too bad, as his next bite is bigger.

"And?" I ask, curious. "How is it?"

"Odd combo. Takes some getting used to, but it's not as bad as I thought." He takes another bite and mumbles with a full mouth, "Actually, it's pretty tasty."

I knew it! "You just have to give peanut butter a fair shot, and it'll win you over. For life."

My enthusiasm makes him smile, and soon the sandwich is gone.

"Want another one?" I ask, still hungry myself.

North looks genuinely happy and nods, so I whip up two more sandwiches, this time one for each of us. Setting his plate and a napkin on the table where he's taken a seat, I'm pleased when he dives in.

"Did I always eat it like this before?" he wonders.

"Nope." I flash a mischievous grin and sit across from him. "Last time I served it to you like this, you spat the first bite into the trash and called me a nutty American."

"Dude, what's your deal?!" North bursts out laughing and hurls the crumpled napkin at me, feigning outrage. I just have to move my shoulder slightly, and it sails past me. "Are you running some weird experiments on me, Dr. Frankenstein?"

"Your memory loss has to have some perks," I retort, sticking my tongue out at him, grinning.

I can't help but feel a pang of sadness as I realize he can recall the stories of Cinderella and Frankenstein's Monster, but not our own. Dr. Curtis at the hospital had mentioned that North's amnesia seemed to affect only the social parts of his brain, leaving the rest untouched. It looks like he was right.

As we opt for a third round of sandwiches, and I find myself playing chef for the evening, I quickly sneak a glance over my shoulder before asking North, "Peanut butter or no?"

He scrunches his brow in thought for a moment

before rolling his eyes and saying, "Ah, screw it! Slather it on."

Oh, how badly I want to yank him by the collar of his hoodie and kiss him right now!

Once our ravenous appetites have been tamed, I stash the sandwich fixings back in the fridge, and we head upstairs together. As North veers into his room, I continue down the hall, but pause to offer a suggestion. "Try *WickedFireflies21*. Your hockey team meant a lot to you. Maybe your password's related to that."

One hand on the doorknob, North takes a moment to process this before his lips curve into a small smile. "Alright. I'll give it a shot." He opens the door but lingers in the doorway for a beat. "Thanks, Adrian," he calls, his crooked grin accompanied by an eye roll. "Also for the bizarre grub."

"No problem," I reply, stepping into my room. But I can't help adding, without peeking back into the hallway, "Give it two days, and you'll be a peanut butter junkie, too."

His warm laughter echoes behind me as I shut the door.

7. Every rose has its thorn

My mind's been on replay all morning, rehashing last night. I almost blew it when I touched his scar, but North seemed open to so much. Could it be too early to hope for a chance to rebuild that incredible connection we once had?

Hope's a risky game, with my heart on the line. But as I scatter fresh straw and hay in the stable, a grin sneaks onto my face. North ate peanut butter. And he hugged me yesterday. That's gotta mean something, right?

When Dr. George Alexander Valentine swings by the farm around ten, I give him a distant wave, not planning on spilling the beans about our forest escapade. Maybe someday, if he's asking again, but for now, it's a hauntingly beautiful memory I'm not ready to share.

As the doc departs, another car I've never seen pulls up—a blue Mercedes sporting white lettering on the sides: *Bower & Klein Insurance Agency.* Oh, right. The insurance ordeal. North was still snoozing when I began my chores, and though I'm dying to see him, it's probably best I'm tied up for a bit. The house is bustling, and I don't want to overwhelm him. Especially since Maddie called to say she's dropping by after lunch to see her long-lost best friend, under the guise of tidying up the house.

Post-shower and seated across from North at lunch, I relish the moment. My heart's so full it feels like it might burst out of my chest and onto the table if I open my mouth too wide. I told him yesterday we'd head out after lunch. That means I'll spend the next few hours with him, and there's no escape to his room. I just need to wait for Maddie. She deserves that.

"Any luck with the password?" I ask between bites, craving the sound of his voice. His presence at today's meal has Ruth humming with delight as she serves up cherry pie. And I can't help but share her happiness. We're both on this journey with North, though our goals differ. She wants her grandson back. I want my boyfriend.

"No, not yet," North replies. "But I'll try a few more similar word combos later. I think you were onto something."

"Oh yeah? Why's that?" I grab a glass, fill it with water under the tap, and take a sip.

"Fireflies must've played a huge part in my life, and not just 'cause of the team. There's a note on my desk covered in firefly stickers. Know anything about it?"

I choke, spraying water into the sink. Holy crap! "Ugh. No idea." Coughing, I wipe my mouth with my sleeve.

"Hey! You okay?" Ruth asks, concern etched on her face as she gently pats my back. "Did you choke?"

"Yeah," I rasp. "Bug in the water."

"Or maybe a firefly?" North teases, shoveling cherry pie into his mouth with a daring glance. Whether he's joking or sizing me up to crack the code of his former life is anyone's guess.

From this point on, I opt for silence and focus on my dessert. Avoiding eye contact, I use the opportunity to wash the dishes.

Just as I finish, I spot the familiar old Volvo of the Brunswick girls rolling up outside the window, its exhaust fumes like a battle cry. I dry my hands on a dish towel and meet Maddie at the door. Her excitement has her pulse racing, making her carotid artery twitch as if she's stuck her finger into a plug socket.

I briefly drape an arm around her neck in greeting and close the door to keep out the chilly winter air. "Is North home?" she whispers in my ear.

Right on cue, we hear his footsteps on the stairs, and I step aside so the two of them can reunite after all this time. Tense, my heart pounds in my throat. Ruth lingers nervously in the doorway between the kitchen and living room. We watch intently for even the slightest reaction from North, hoping Maddie's presence might spark a memory. Anything.

He's been warned that the housemaid is coming today, so he's not too surprised when he sees her. But there's no sign of recognition on his face. "Hi," he says calmly, taking a few steps toward her as she stands rooted to the spot. "You're Madelyn, right?"

Her lower lip and chin start to quiver. What the hell is happening now? Seemingly unable to find her voice, she just nods. And then the usually composed Canadian girl starts to cry as if North had stashed chopped onions in his pockets. She tries to maintain her composure, but tears stream silently down her cheeks.

This isn't the reunion we'd pictured, especially not Maddie.

"Hey...why are you crying?" North asks, a fair question since, in his mind, she's only here to help Ruth with housekeeping. We didn't want to reveal their true connection just yet. But his words sound tender, as if he'd seen through the ruse from the get-go.

"It's just...the cold," Madelyn stammers, hastily wiping away her tears. "I'm allergic, you know?"

"To snow?" he questions, raising an eyebrow skeptically, but his voice lacks any cynical accusation.

Instead, he surprises us all by closing the gap between them and enveloping her in a warm hug. "I guess, under different circumstances," he murmurs softly into her hair, "I'd probably say: *it's nice to see you again.*"

Yeah, no doubt he would. He'd also catch her and twirl her around as she squealed with delight, rushing toward him.

Maddie clings to his white long-sleeved shirt, which has completely thrown me off today because of its color, and dabs her tear-streaked eyes on his shoulder. "How are you?" she sniffles afterward.

North loosens his hold on the petite girl a bit and offers her a smile. "I'm doing well. Every day there are a few new surprises, but I can handle it."

It's obvious to Madelyn that her emotional outburst was one of those surprises, so she bravely lets go of him, sniffs one last time, and manages a confident, dazzling smile. "Well, that's good." She takes a step back and regains her composure. "Adrian mentioned you guys are heading to town today. You should probably get going."

North gives a slight nod. "I guess we'll cross paths later."

No doubt. I can't see Maddie ending the day without seeing him again. But she could use some alone time to process the whirlwind of emotions that just hit her.

Ruth's already slipped back into the kitchen, likely because the tender moment between them brought tears to her eyes. I won't lie, my own throat tightened up, too. Inhaling deeply to shake off the lingering tension, I call out, "Ruth, we're heading out! Need anything from town?"

"No, thank you. We're all set," she answers from the kitchen. "Have fun, you two!" I catch the faint waver in her voice that she's been trying to mask lately.

As North and I lace up our shoes and make for the door, Madelyn stands behind the couch, looking a bit dazed. "Catch you later," I mouth to her, silently but firmly reassuring her that she should definitely wait for us. It'll be good for all of us to hang out a bit.

After that emotional rollercoaster, it's tough to get back to the easy banter North and I shared in the kitchen last night. But as we hit the road, I make a conscious effort to loosen up. I don't want to sit beside him in the car, which I'm driving today, all stiff and tense. "How'd it go with the insurance agent?" I ask, breaking the silence that's been riding shotgun since the car radio's on the fritz.

"Pretty well, I think," he says, his voice betraying little emotion. He's probably lost in thought. Then, clearing his throat, he continues more earnestly, "Turns out my car was pretty new and well-insured. The agent wired thirty-eight grand to my account today. Can you believe it?"

Holy cow!

"That's a sweet stack of cash," I reply, mirroring his earlier nonchalance. "Wow."

"Yeah. And there's more." With his head resting on the headrest, North shifts his gaze to me. "My college ice hockey team had extra accident insurance for hospital stays, follow-up care, and a bunch of other stuff the guy mentioned. In the next few weeks, I'll get about half of that amount on top of what I already got."

"Damn! Are you serious?" I exclaim, turning to stare at him for a second.

He shrugs and pulls a cynical face that makes my stomach twist. "I'm one lucky son of a gun."

Crap. I can't even begin to imagine what's going through his mind. So many people dream of a windfall like that. But money will never make up for what he's lost.

North lets out a deep sigh beside me, and I know exactly what he's doing. He's swallowing the heavy atmosphere and putting on a brave face. But the fact that it's all just an act is painfully clear, making me want to pull over and shake some sense into him.

"You don't have to pretend everything's okay," I tell him, my voice lower than before. "Just be honest when you're feeling like crap."

"It'd break the old lady's heart," North murmurs, turning his head to the window. "And something tells me it'd hurt the housekeeper, too."

The weight of his burden slams into me like a wrecking ball. It's terrible that he, of all people—trapped in this heartbreaking situation feels responsible for the well-being of others. How long until he reaches his breaking point?

A suffocating sensation tightens around my chest, so I'm relieved when we finally arrive in town and step out of the car in front of the electronics store. The crisp air helps clear the gloomy atmosphere, even though it already carries the scent of the snow that's bound to fall again soon.

North takes his time selecting a new phone in the store, even asking for my opinion before making a decision. But as soon as he's found, bought, and stashed away his new gadget, and we're back at Ruth's old pick-up, I'm hit with a wave of disappointment that we didn't take longer. Somehow, I'd had this bizarre idea of an extended shopping trip when he'd asked me to tag along yesterday. Sadly, Moonbreak Falls isn't exactly a shopping mecca.

On the other hand, North looks just as unsatisfied as I feel, so I suggest, "Wanna explore town some more?"

I haven't even finished my sentence when he spins around, eyes lit up, and exclaims an enthusiastic "Yes!" right in my face.

I grin in response, slip the car keys back into my jacket pocket, and veer left with North by my side. There's not much to see here, but we frequently pause at storefronts, and I give him all the time he needs to take in his hometown. It also gives me the chance to observe him quietly.

Though I started off leading the way, I soon get caught up in North's curiosity and stroll leisurely beside him as he chooses our path. "Oh, check that out," he exclaims excitedly as we cross a street, pointing diagonally ahead with an outstretched arm. "What a charming diner. You ever been there?"

My blood rushes unexpectedly as I hadn't realized where we'd ended up. "Yeah," I reply tersely.

"And?"

"And what?" If he suggests grabbing a cupcake right now, my nerves won't take it.

"How's the food?"

I shrug, eyes downcast, silently urging North to move on. "It's good."

Of course, I couldn't have been more obvious in my attempt to steer him away without him noticing my eagerness to leave this spot. "So, no milkshake then," he concludes, stopping dead in his tracks, making a point.

Crap!

I halt, sigh deeply, and turn to face him. Silently, I shake my head.

"Why not?" he asks, now clearly determined to get to the truth. He even crosses his arms as if to show I won't be escaping this situation easily. "Am I in for another surprise inside? A waitress who's more than just a waitress?" His reference to Maddie as a maid is a bullseye. Our secrecy must have hurt him more than we initially thought.

I shake my head again, but this time sincerely, because I don't think he shared a deeper connection with any of the diner's waitresses.

"Then what? Were we ever there together?" he prods further. "Is it a bad memory?"

And now, I'm at a loss for words. Unable to respond with even a shake of my head, I avoid his gaze, staring down at the ground.

"Oh God. We *were* there together..." he murmurs, his voice suddenly so understanding that it breaks my heart. "Weren't we?"

Reluctantly, I meet his eyes, where countless connections are trying to form.

"And they're not bad memories. They're good ones." Overwhelmed by a truth he doesn't even know, his arms drop wearily. "You said we're friends. We probably hung out there often in the past, sharing great times together."

Just once. But it was beautiful.

The fact that he's not entirely accurate about the diner reassures me a bit, but it doesn't lift the heaviness in my chest.

North abandons his attempts to provoke me, joins me at my side, and we walk a few quiet steps together. Then, suddenly, with sincerity and unmistakable remorse in his words, he says, "It must be tough for you to be around me right now. You...with all these cherished memories of our friendship. And me...with nothing left."

"No!" I spin around to face him. "No, that's not it at all!" Jeez, when will this ever end? I don't want him to feel bad because of me. Groaning, I rub my face and then firmly grasp his arms. "Listen, I love spending time with you. Whether you remember our past or not doesn't matter. Because even if you've forgotten some things for now, you're still—*well I don't know!*" I shrug and glance at the cloud-covered sky for guidance. "Just *you.*" The mood is getting too serious, and I don't want to risk it spiraling downward, so I muster all my strength and force a playful smile, as difficult as it is, like doing a hundred pull-ups in a row. But I manage. And then I add, "As long as you keep letting me carry out some wild experiments with you, everything's okay."

That earns me a small smile from him, and I breathe a sigh of relief.

"And now, come on!" I say, looping my arm casually around his neck, so no one who doesn't know the truth would think anything of it. "You wanted to see the town, so let's keep going before people think we're lost and offer us a place to stay." I tug him along for a few steps, then we turn right at the end of the street and stroll on with our hands in our jacket pockets.

One minute later, North stops, throws his arm in front of my stomach, and gasps, "You know what?"

"What?" I groan, the abrupt halt stealing my breath.

His eyes light up with that adventurous twinkle again, making him look much younger than twenty-one for a moment. "Let's do something crazy!"

I'm in! "What do you have in mind?" I ask, swept up in his enthusiasm.

"No idea!" And just like that, our adventure seems to have reached its end.

But I don't want him to lose his excitement so quickly, so I glance around for help. And there's something. I bite my lower lip because it's a bit much, but...why not?

North notices where I'm looking and turns in that direction along with me. For three seconds, we both stare at the gleaming black BMW X5 showcased under the spotlights at *Oliver's Used Cars*. A grin, born from the depths of pure mischief, spreads across North's face, and he growls daringly, "Oh yeah... Let's buy a car!"

8. The truth is down the hallway to the left

North should have memorized the way to the farm by now, still I lead the way as he tails me in his sleek, raven-black BMW. I can practically see his proud grin in my rearview mirror.

We park one after the other, and I can't help but smile watching North admire his new prize with pure joy. The SUV is a stunner, fitting North like a glove. While he heads inside, I grab the horses from the paddock and rush to catch up.

Barging through the door, I nearly cause a living room pile-up. North stands frozen, under the shocked gaze of two wide-eyed women. Then their frantic eyes turn to me, and Maddie explodes, "You let him buy a car?"

I absorb the scolding for a second before confidently standing by North. Leaning casually against him, I rest my left elbow on his right shoulder, cross one leg in front of the other, and flash a devilish grin at the ladies. "Oh yeah! And you wouldn't believe the thrill it was!" I fire back.

Out of the corner of my eye, I catch North's lips curving mischievously as he folds his arms, ready for battle, and throws me a reckless, but invigorating sideways glance. This moment alone made it all worth it.

"Well?" he dares the two stunned women. "You gonna stand here until the cows come home, or are you coming out to check out my sweet new ride?"

They can't resist his invitation and, despite shaking their heads, follow him outside. It takes no time at all for Maddie's indignant shriek to reach me in the cozy parlor. "A BMW? *Adrian!*"

Laughing, I head to the kitchen and sit at the table with a glass of juice, waiting for the others to return—Maddie's in shock, Ruth is clearly impressed, and North is beaming. I suggest a poker game to wrap up the day with friends, setting the mood just right.

"If you win, I might let you drive my new car," North teases Maddie, acting like it's no big deal. We all hold our breath during moments like these, although we really should get over it. Just because his personality is still the same doesn't mean we'll have the old North back anytime soon. But I'm digging the new one, too.

"Don't say that!" I warn him quickly, snatching the playing cards from the living room sideboard and plopping down in my kitchen chair. "She had a lucky streak last time, and technically, she already *owns* the BMW."

"Is that so...?" North murmurs, leaning roguishly toward Madelyn, propped up on both elbows. "And how does a housemaid end up gambling so much cash with her employer?"

If I didn't know better, I'd say he's flirting with her.

Damn it. I don't know better. The thought makes my stomach twist.

"Because said employer, when they were little, torched her brand-new doll's hair. She's had free rein ever since," Maddie shoots back with a smug grin that suits her way more than tears.

We can almost hear the gears turning in North's head, but Madelyn doesn't share any more childhood tales. Instead, she puts on her poker face and coolly declares, "Alright, boys. Let's play!"

Ruth retreats to the living room with Elvis Presley, claiming God won't let her into his gambling-free heaven if she sticks with the sinful crowd in the kitchen. No biggie. Taking money from an old lady isn't our style anyway. But Madelyn has no problem taking us boys for all we're worth. After an hour, North calls it quits, joking, "Before I lose the house and the farm."

"We could switch it up," she teases, grinning mischievously. "How about Ludo, but we'll need a bottle of vodka, and you gotta be a hard-core drinker. You still got that in you, North?"

"Jeez," he chuckles, rising from his chair. "What kind of friends did I have in my past life?"

"Only the best," Madelyn playfully wiggles her eyebrows. But we let North go as he wants to set up his new phone. Apparently, he found the PIN code for his SIM card among his stuff in a drawer yesterday.

As he heads upstairs, I shuffle the cards and deal them just for the wild Canadian and me. She takes the chance to whisper softly, "He's looking good. Relaxed, right? How's he holding up?"

"Sometimes good, sometimes not so much," I admit. "There're moments when it feels like he's right there with me, just like before. And then there're times when I wish I could take away all the pain he's hiding."

She nods somberly and seems a bit guilty. "Guess my surprise visit this afternoon didn't help much, huh?"

We both trade the cards we can't use in the game. Maddie takes two and I deal myself three new ones, leaving me with two jacks and two aces. "It threw him off for a bit," I reveal. "But I think he values having you as a poker buddy more than just watching you from a distance with the mop."

"We should've been upfront with him from the

start," she concedes. "He took the news that we've been friends for ages pretty well after all."

At least it seemed that way.

I wish I could tell him the truth about us, too. But that's a whole different story from the thing with Maddie.

Playing cards with only two people isn't all that fun, and the little Canadian wins again with three queens. I toss my cards onto the table and lean back, interlacing my fingers behind my neck as I study the ceiling. "Do you think someone's sexual orientation can change because of memory loss?"

"You mean if he's not into guys anymore?"

I nod.

"Honestly, I'm clueless." She shrugs and makes a thoughtful face. "In high school, he was open to both for a while, until he finally chose guys around eighteen or nineteen. Maybe he needs to go through that journey again to figure out where his heart truly lies."

Her prediction is disheartening, and she can clearly see it on my face.

Quickly, she leans in and pats my arm. "Don't stress. It won't be that bad. And who knows, he might get his memory back in just two or three days."

That shred of hope is killing me! Sometimes I think it'd be more realistic to accept that his memories may never return, but I can't embrace that idea just yet.

"Come on! Let's go check on him," she suggests.

"He'll have plenty of time to be alone later." With a sigh, I push myself up from the table. As she follows me upstairs, she asks, "Did you guys visit the horses yet? Maybe riding through the woods or just racing around the pasture would help him."

I glance back at her. "You think he can still do it?"

"It's possible. He didn't forget how to drive a car, after all."

As I reach the top and turn the corner, I halt abruptly, and Maddie bumps into me. "What's up?" she grumbles, then spots North in the hallway outside his room and blurts out a surprised, "Hi."

North gazes at me with such distance, as if we hadn't spent half the afternoon together in the kitchen, conspiring to beat Madelyn at poker so we wouldn't lose our last shirts to her. In fact, he stares at both of us that intently. Then he focuses solely on her, and that dreadful uncertainty creeps back into his eyes, which always knocks me off balance.

Maddie gulps beside me.

"Are you my girlfriend?" he finally asks with the vulnerability of a lost boy seeking his way home.

"What? *No!*" she replies quickly. *Too* quickly. "What gave you that idea?"

Then North lifts his phone, now working flawlessly, and holds the colorful display out to us.

"Fuck," I mutter in a hushed whisper, and I

instinctively take a small step back. *Fuck! Fuck! Fuck!* Why didn't I think of the photos?

"If you're not my girlfriend," he groans, nearly breaking, "why are there so many pictures of you kissing me?"

"Because—"

Well, what now, Maddie?

She sighs. "We used to be together, but that was a long time ago."

"The pictures are from mid-December."

"Yeah, exactly...that's how long ago it was."

Oh God, Madelyn! What are you doing? My shocked gaze flicks to her for a split second, then back to North.

A hundred gears click together behind his puzzled eyes, but I don't think they're getting this vehicle anywhere close to running. Though he opens his mouth, he closes it again without speaking and furrows his brow in deep thought. He wants so many answers, and I wish we could give them to him. But if Dr. Curtis is right, it will only make things worse. I don't want North to pull away from me. Not now, when he's just starting to open up.

All three of us stand rooted in the hallway, like a sad little cluster of trees. Only North looks like he's just been chopped down.

"Why did we break up?" he nearly pleads with

Maddie, desperate to finally unlock the mystery of his past.

She takes a small step toward him and raises her hands. But she lets them drop again without touching him, instead placing a hand on her heart. Maybe to comfort herself. "Because we're not meant for each other," she whispers.

Now it's North who reaches for her hand and intertwines his fingers with hers, just like he's done with me a couple of times before. My breath catches, but I bite my tongue until my vision blurs with tiny tears of pain.

"Did I mess up?" he asks her, so genuinely sad and remorseful that any girl in the world would have taken him back in that moment—if the story Maddie had spun were true.

"Jesus Christ, no! You didn't do anything wrong," she assures him, placing her free hand on his cheek. "*North*— You're the most amazing person I know."

"Then why? Did you leave me for someone else?" Technically, he's only known her since this afternoon. Why on Earth does he sound so heartbroken, as if this is tearing him apart?

Madelyn shakes her head with a heartfelt exhale. "We just don't work together. Not in that way."

North's shoulders slump in defeat. He takes one last look at the phone before putting it back in his pocket. "I don't understand any of this."

"I know, sweetheart," she replies empathetically,

pressing her petite body against his in a loving embrace. "Someday you'll understand again, but for now, don't worry about it. Please! Everything is fine between us." As he hesitantly wraps his arms around her and rests his cheek on her head for a moment, she closes her eyes with a touch of sadness. "We've always worked best as friends. That's all we need."

"Okay…" he murmurs, blinking slowly and looking completely bewildered at me. But all I can offer him is a helpless shrug.

When she's ready, Maddie disentangles herself from him and takes a deep breath. "I should go now." She smiles up at his face with a heartwarming softness. "But it was really nice to see you again."

"It was nice to meet you, too," he replies.

And then Maddie rolls her eyes so adorably at this absurd situation and shakes her head that I almost have to laugh in despair. She stands on her tiptoes and gives him a small farewell kiss on the cheek. "Take care, North," she says with a now much steadier voice. In the next second, she leaves him behind and hurries down the stairs.

I accompany her to the door, feeling utterly overwhelmed, puffing the breath out of my bloated cheeks. How is this all supposed to go on?

As she slips on her jacket in the living room to the music of Elvis Presley, I lean back against the edge of the dresser with my hands in my pockets. *"We were together, but we broke up before Christmas?"* I whisper quietly enough that Ruth doesn't hear us from her rocking chair. "That's probably the lamest excuse you could come up with."

"What do you think I should've said?" she hisses back. "The truth about you can be found down the hall on the left?"

That's where my room is. No, that probably wouldn't have been a better solution either.

Madelyn zips up her jacket, places her hands on my chest, and gazes at me intently. "Take care of him, Adrian." With that, she closes this chapter of today's escapade and calls out over my shoulder, "Good night, Ruth!"

"Get home safe, dear!" comes the reply from the fireplace as I already let her out into the dark.

As soon as I close the door behind her, I rub my face with both hands and nearly claw the flesh from my bones with my fingers.

Argh!

9. Peanut butter sandwiches

North doesn't reappear downstairs that evening, so around ten, I escape to my room, eager to put this rollercoaster of a day behind me. Before snuggling into bed, though, I flop down on my mattress and dial Sandy, responding to her text from a few minutes ago asking for an update on our situation.

What starts as a brief check-in turns into a forty-five-minute heart-to-heart, as I spill more than I intended. Unburdening my concerns feels like a weight lifted off my chest, though. Just as Sandy sends her support from Portland, an unexpected knock sounds at my door, and I glance up, startled. One second later, North hesitantly peeks into my room and inquires, "Can I come in?"

"Uh, yeah, sure," I mumble, then hurriedly tell Sandy, "I'll call you back tomorrow. Something's come up." Too preoccupied to say goodnight, I drop my phone into my lap and disconnect the call. "What's up?" I ask North, giving him my undivided attention.

He's already stepped into my room, slouching slightly, balancing a plate stacked high with sandwiches. Roast beef and lettuce peek out from between the bread, accompanied by the occasional cucumber slice. "I can't sleep. You hungry?"

His abrupt shift in topic puzzles me, but I nod and slide back toward my headboard, clearing a spot for him to sit.

With a hint of shyness, North perches at the foot of the bed and crosses his legs. We face each other like two kids at a sleepover, the plate of sandwiches acting as a makeshift campfire between us. Unable to resist my curiosity, I lift the top slice of bread from a sandwich and, to my delight, I discover he even slathered on peanut butter!

Feeling a surge of energy, I grab the top sandwich, and North's grin widens as he reaches for the second one.

We savor the first few bites in silence, but North can't keep quiet for long—a fact I'm grateful for. His voice is like music to my ears. "Today was super intense," he kicks off the conversation.

"Exhausting?"

"Mm-hmm."

"Yet you can't sleep?"

With a sigh, he shakes his head, avoiding my eyes for the first time since entering the room. "During the day, it's not so bad. But at night, when everything's silent, that's when it starts—"

"What does?" I prod, as he'd trails off.

North toys with a lettuce leaf in his sandwich, as if gathering his thoughts. "You know that feeling when you can't quite recall something, but you're sure you know it? Like it's just beyond your reach, and you can't quite grab it?"

I know precisely what he means.

With the vulnerability of a lost boy abandoned by Peter Pan on a pirate ship, he lifts his eyes to meet mine from beneath his lashes and bangs. "I've felt like that ever since I woke up. Constantly."

Oh man. "That sucks." Finishing my snack, I lean back and stretch out, crossing my legs next to his knee and clasping my hands on my stomach. "Can't you distract yourself with something?"

"What do you think I'm doing here?" His sly grin makes me smile, too.

Right.

"Any luck with your computer?"

With a shake of his head, North stands, carrying the

nearly empty plate to my desk. His black gloves lie there, practically begging him to put them on. I watch, captivated, as he slides them on one by one and then examines his hands. They stand out against his white long-sleeved shirt, making my throat go dry.

Intrigued, he faces me. "Did I wear these a lot?"

"Almost always." Damn, but my voice is strained.

His attention returns to his hands, flexing and stretching his fingers. "They feel good. Comfortable. And somehow...familiar." That last word sends my heart racing, but I quickly squash any rising hopes. I must have made a sound, though, because North turns and studies me. "You wish I could remember..." he says softly.

"We all wish you could remember."

"And what if I never do?"

"Then you have a whole life ahead of you to make new memories." Miraculously, I manage to sound more at ease than I feel. Taking advantage of my composure, I steer the conversation casually. "Find anything useful on your phone?"

"Just pics of friends at college, some selfies, and a few short videos of my hockey team's games." His eyes drift to my bulletin board, where only a photo of Sandy, me, and my mom remain. "Apparently, I was in a *Fireflies* WhatsApp group," he continues, absentminded. "Messages keep coming in. I said a quick hello, and they all freaked out, sending me like a hundred private messages within minutes. It got overwhelming, so I backed off. Guess, I'll just call some of those guys tomorrow."

I can only imagine the shock his message must have caused. Feeling sorry for his friends waiting for more news from North, I'm also grateful he's chosen to spend time in my room instead.

His gaze lands on my drawings, untouched since yesterday. He's seen them all before, but he flips through them again anyway. Occasionally, his eyes dart to the pin board, comparing the drawn Sandy to the real one. "Is that your girlfriend?" he inquires.

"She's a friend. But not the girl I love."

In an *aha*-gesture, he nods. Leaving the drawings, his attention shifts to his black hoodie draped over the chair. He picks it up, sliding it on and zipping it halfway. Looking down, he assesses himself.

My heart clenches.

Closing my eyes briefly, I'm overwhelmed by how much I've missed him looking like this. When the mattress dips as he sits down, I open my eyes again. "What's the name of the girl you love?" North asks, his gaze locked on mine.

I study him, wishing I could freeze this moment and keep him here forever.

Finally, I whisper, "There is no girl."
Just you.

"Ah... That's too bad," he states calmly, then

hesitates and adds, without committing to a solid opinion, "Or maybe not."

His endearing confusion makes me smile. "It's fine the way it is." The topic stirs another emotion in me, and I can't help but ask, "So, what was the deal with you and Madelyn today? It almost seemed like you were regretting not being together. Did you want her to be your girlfriend?"

Once the words leave my lips, I brace myself for his response.

North studies me for so long that goosebumps prickle my arms. What the hell is going on behind those deep blue eyes? Finally, he sighs, letting go of whatever thoughts are swirling inside him. "No, I'm glad things are the way they are. I haven't known her for even a day, but I can see why I liked her before. But honestly, handling a girlfriend right now would be too much."

I can live with that answer—and thankfully, I can breathe again. "So, what was bothering you?"

"I don't know." He frowns and shrugs. "She's such a great girl. I guess I just didn't want to be the jerk who hurt her."

"You could never."

"Hurt her?"

"Be a jerk."

"So, I was a nice guy before?" Two dimples grace his cheeks, and I think the idea pleases him.

"From what I've seen, you were one of the nicest people on Earth."

"Wow," he says dryly. "No pressure there."

"That's not what I meant." Laughing out loud, I roll my eyes. "You don't have to try to be exactly like you were before. Just be yourself. Whatever feels natural."

"Sometimes, it's really hard," he murmurs, his gaze dropping to his fidgeting fingers. "I wish I could get my past back. Without it, I feel so incredibly empty."

"Hey, don't get gloomy now!" I scold playfully, tossing my pillow at his face. "The night is still young, and we're way too sober for that."

North holds my pillow, hugging it like a teddy bear. Meanwhile, I slide back to lean against the headboard.

"I'm probably just high from all the peanut butter," he jokes, trying to lighten the mood.

"See?" I stick my tongue out at him. "I knew you'd become a junkie once you gave the stuff a real chance."

Resting his chin on the pillow he still cradles, North grins. "Are you an optimist, Adrian?" Although his voice carries a hint of sadness, there's also a glimmer of hope. It's a potent combination that gets under my skin.

"When it comes to you, yes," I assure him.

His eyes narrow with curiosity. "Am I an optimist, too?"

"You definitely used to be."

"So we keep believing that my twenty-one previous

years haven't completely vanished?"

"Absolutely!" I wish I could hug him right now and promise that his life will be wonderful again soon. "Maybe your memory will return not in a massive wave, but in small bursts. Just like your own character has been emerging more and more. And we'll make every step back into your past a glimmer of hope."

"Yes, let's do that." With sudden confidence, North smiles and nods as if this were our secret, the rest of the world irrelevant in our private bubble. Then he begins to hum a soft melody, swaying gently as he still hugs my pillow like a security blanket.

And my blood runs cold.

"What are you doing?" I whisper, barely audible.

He blinks twice, just as puzzled as I am, then shrugs one shoulder, cradling the pillow in one arm and pulling his smartphone from his pocket with the other. As he taps the screen, searching for something, he murmurs, "I don't know. I've had this melody with a few lines in my head for days." He types something, likely searching the web or YouTube while quietly humming the song. "Ah. There's something."

But I knew what he was looking for before he even started.

"Afterglow," we say together—he with curiosity, I softly, caught in a whirlpool of emotions.

As the song begins playing from North's phone,

filling my room with a gentle melody, my world trembles.

"You know this song?" he asks, focusing on my undoubtedly pale face.

"Yes…" My voice is barely a croak. "It was playing that night in your car."

Instantly, North understands what's affecting me so deeply, and it seems like he just needs to make a small adjustment within himself to join me in my world. "You mean, on the drive through the forest?"

I manage a slight nod. "It was the last thing you heard before the accident." And the first thing I heard after coming to.

For an endless moment, we stare at each other across my bed. Until suddenly, North starts to smile—a beautiful sight I haven't seen in weeks. And I know where it comes from; I feel it within myself, too.

With eyes shining like stars, he excitedly slaps his right hand onto my outstretched leg, just above my knee. "So this is our first glimmer of hope?"

My grin widens, and I place my hand on top of his. "Yes. It is." My fingers slip between his without thinking. Oh, how much I long to grip his hand tighter and pull him closer—close enough to feel his lips on mine again.

At that thought, my heart races wildly.

It takes a moment, but then North seems to notice our hand position, too. However, it doesn't bring him the same joy it does me. At best, he's surprised or even thrown off. His smile fades, and his eyebrows lower just enough to reveal confusion. Carefully, he withdraws his hand.

Why so agonizingly slow?

It almost feels like he's unsure whether to leave his hand there or pull it away. The uncertainty threatens to be my undoing tonight!

Once again, North wraps both arms around my pillow as he avoids my gaze. "I should probably go now and let you sleep," he says calmly but suddenly distant, as if we have lost our connection. "You have to get up early tomorrow, and I've already kept you awake too long."

No, don't go!

But I don't know how to stop him. North is already standing with my pillow in his arm. He places it on my stomach, but as a parting gesture, he offers a barely-there smile. Hidden behind it are indecisive thoughts he no longer shares with me. "Thanks for the distraction, Adrian."

Sighing, I nod. "Sleep well, North."

He quietly leaves my room, the last sandwich still on my desk.

10. Half-truths for breakfast

The enigmatic depth in North's eyes before he disappeared through the door haunted my sleepless night. A fierce inner battle waged within me, torn between wondering if North found the touch of our hands on my thigh repugnant or if, just maybe, he relished it even for a fleeting moment. His guarded gaze revealed nothing, leaving me in a maddening state of uncertainty.

When my alarm rudely interrupts the next morning, I groggily roll out of bed, like I do every day on the farm, wash and get dressed, then trudge downstairs. I lug in an armful of firewood before pouring myself a potent coffee in the kitchen, hoping to quell last night's relentless thoughts. The only exception from routine is North, already sitting at the kitchen table, greeting me with a contemplative silence.

"Whoa," escapes my lips in surprise, and I approach the coffee machine with a puzzled furrow in my brow. "Why are you up so early?"

"Early is relative. I haven't slept at all."

Oh, no! A tidal wave of sympathy crashes over me as I load the old coffee maker with fragrant grounds. Of course. North had been grappling with his own demons last night. He'd told me. It also explains why he's still clad in yesterday's clothes, fingerless gloves and all.

"You could've stayed last night," I say without turning to face him.

"Yeah, I know," comes his response, laced with a sigh. "But not the whole night."

It's all about perspective.

"Do you want some coffee, too?" I offer as a diversion, already adding extra water to the machine before flipping the switch. Glancing up, I find him suddenly beside me, leaning against the kitchen counter, nodding wordlessly.

His unexpected proximity makes me swallow and instinctively retreat half a step. Heck, why did I do this when in truth I don't want any distance between us at all.

My gaze, lost in thought, must have lingered on North a second too long because he narrows his eyes and tilts his head, asking, "What's up?"

"Nothing." To dodge the moment, I snatch two mugs and Ruth's new sugar bowl from the shelf, laying out a spoon and grabbing the milk as well.

North remains rooted, tracking my movements with his eyes until I perch on the counter, legs dangling. We wait together for the dark brew to finish dripping, our gazes seemingly fused by an unbreakable bond. My pulse quickens, feeling the swarm of fireflies in my stomach urging me to fall head over heels for North Beckett once more, from the tip of his perfect nose to the enigma behind the oceanic depths of his eyes. I struggle to maintain steady breaths, focusing on each inhale, unable to bear his piercing gaze any longer. He, too, leans against the counter, fingers gripping the edge, as if seeking additional support.

The silence between us swells, consuming the room until my ears buzz with its intensity. Neither of us has blinked in the last fifteen seconds.

What's happening here?

"Adrian...?" North finally murmurs when the coffee pot has long been filled, and we're still locked in our motionless stare.

"Hm?"

"Can I ask you a question?"

By now, he knows he can ask me anything. But his choice of words suggests something significant is coming.

A tingle creeps up the back of my neck. "Of course."

"Before the accident—" He pauses briefly. "We didn't know each other very long then, right? You said, two weeks, or something."

I nod.

"Is it possible—and please don't take this the wrong way—but..." North's eyes narrow ever so slightly, and he licks his lips. "Were you maybe a little infatuated with me?"

My heart lurches to a stop, and my expression falls. I was prepared for many things, but not this. Then again...this is just North. Candid. Direct. No detours.

"Oh my God!" I exclaim, laughing uncontrollably at his frankness. "How could anyone take that the wrong way?"

North's smile emerges. My ability to jest about it and not react defensively seems to surprise him.

It surprises me, too. But the past few weeks have been grueling, and I've hit my limit. I loathe this cat-and-mouse game. Even if I can't reveal a sliver of the truth about him, me, us, and eternity, it feels liberating to let the turmoil in my head run wild for a moment.

"And, were you?" he presses, a crooked grin playing on his lips, mirrored by my own. I find his curiosity about my feelings—even if not about his own—undeniably alluring.

"Possibly..." I purr, an uninhibited daring in my

tone that borders on a challenge.

North accepts the invitation to this bold conversation. He studies me silently for several seconds, fingers drumming on the underside of the counter. In his smoldering gaze, the next question takes shape like a mischievous thought.

"Did I notice that before?" he inquires, and I grant him the satisfaction of a nod. His eyebrows dip playfully, and he bites his lower lip slyly. "Did you ever hit on me?"

Glancing at the ceiling, I exhale a soft chuckle. "*Nooo*, I wouldn't say that." Most advances came from him, and I relished every single one. "Why?" I counter, fearlessly meeting his eyes again. "Do you think maybe you would've wanted that?"

Now it's his turn to snort a small laugh. It's evasive, endearingly sweet, and pauses him just a second too long before responding. I've caught him off guard. "The idea is probably a bit far-fetched," he sidesteps a direct answer.

Is he saying that because he doesn't feel attracted to me or because, in his mind, he was still with Maddie back then?

With a telling expression, I press my lips into a brief smile and playfully echo his own word. "Probably."

As if I've just bewildered him and he doesn't dare admit it, he finally breaks our eye contact and reaches for the coffee pot. But the conversation isn't over. "So, it didn't bother me earlier in our friendship that you had a crush on me?" he asks, concentrating intently on pouring the first cup.

"Does it bother you now?" I counter softly, my heart pounding as I wait for his response.

For a moment, North tilts his head and blinks sideways at me, as if searching for the answer on a painted canvas. Then he gifts me a smile that conveys everything and nothing at all. "No."

I'm losing my mind! Have we just crossed some unspoken threshold, or is he simply cool with me staring at him like he's on the big screen, as long as I keep my distance?

Jeez!

I let out a quiet sigh, barely audible, as I watch North pour coffee into a second mug. He lowers the pot but continues to hold it. A few seconds tick by before I realize he's in a trance-like state, fixated on the two plump ceramic mugs.

"What's up?" I ask, yanked out of the previous moment.

He places the pot back under the machine and turns to face me, genuinely baffled. With his mouth quirked to one side, he rubs his neck. "Do you remember how I used to take my coffee?"

My heart swells—that's so sweet! And pitiful. "Yeah, why?" I chuckle and tease him by sticking my tongue out, payback for earlier. "Don't you?"

"Ha. Ha," North retorts sarcastically, but then grins. "Now help me!"

Actually, I haven't seen him drink coffee since he got back. "How did you take it at the hospital?" I inquire.

"They only had tea."

"*Ugh*, that's rough."

"Adrian!" he growls, impatient for an answer.

I know I shouldn't delight in his predicament, yet I can't help but giggle—his impatience is just so endearing. It might not be exactly the same, but I've definitely missed this. "Okay," I finally give in and slide off the counter. "I have an idea."

He eyes me warily, clearing a small space for me in front of the mugs. "What's your plan?"

"We'll start a new experiment." Grinning, I load one of the cups with milk and sugar to my liking. I leave the second coffee as black as night. Then I present both mugs to North with a flourish. "Discover what you prefer."

In a heartbeat, a mischievous twinkle lights up his eyes. He reaches for the dark, aromatic brew, too bitter for my taste. Cautiously, he takes a small sip, savoring the flavor. Apparently, that's not enough, so he takes a second, slightly larger sip. Swishing it around in his mouth, he finally declares, "Mmh. Not bad." North hands me the cup and grabs the other one. Again, he samples the concoction, but this time he grimaces as if he's swallowed battery acid. "And this is pure sacrilege!"

Amused, we swap cups, and I take a satisfying sip of my sweet coffee to show North he's made the right choice from his perspective.

"Damn, how can you stomach this sugary sludge?" he grumbles indignantly, chasing the taste of my coffee from his tongue with his bitter brew.

"That's rich coming from someone who once made me chug an entire bag of maple syrup with his best friend. Pure!"

North cringes at the image. "God. That's gross."

"Yep." I can't argue with him on that one.

"And you still kept us as friends?"

"It was...for a good reason," I explain, feeling nostalgic. "A sort of initiation into a very unique family." I grab some chocolate cookies from the cupboard and set them on the counter beside us. "Here, try these. You used to love them."

The fact that he doesn't take a dainty nibble, but instead shoves a whole cookie into his mouth, tells me he trusts me, and that feels good. It's also nice to see one cookie after another vanish from the plate, like the Cookie Monster himself has invaded Ruth's kitchen.

Once my coffee cup is empty, I put it in the sink and inform North, "I've gotta head to the stable now." Even though I'd rather stay here longer and work through some stuff with him. "Are you going upstairs to lie down?"

"No, I'm still not tired."

Or not anymore, after that black caffeine potion. I wouldn't be surprised.

"Can I come with you?"

"To the stable?" I ask, surprised.

"Yeah. I wanna know what I used to do every day when I was home." He's already following me through the living room to our boots by the door. "I couldn't have just bummed around all vacation long and let you do all the work, right?"

"No. You weren't lazy." I grab his jacket off the hook and toss it to him. Then I slip into my own. "You usually woke up even before me. We took care of the horses together, did minor repairs around the farm, sometimes you studied for college, and occasionally you restocked the agricultural supplies."

"Okaaay...that sounds like a pretty full day. Did we ever have fun in between?" His eyebrows pull down skeptically as we head across the yard to the barn. "Or is that forbidden for the employees on our farm?"

I can't help but smile, because in truth, the time with North, whether at work or after, was the most beautiful of my life. "We once chopped down a singing tree," I share. "That was fun."

North sighs, not understanding a word, and I teasingly raise my eyebrows, giving him a little challenge. After all, he did the same to me back in the day. I'm just returning the favor with gratitude—and finally understanding why he enjoyed it so much back then.

From the back of the stable, a chorus of horse snorts greets us as soon as we flip on the light. I hand North a few carrots from the large bucket. "Time to say hello to some old friends," I tell him and lead him to the back.

North walks slowly, taking in every detail of the barn. He removes his fingerless gloves and stores them in his jacket pocket before feeding the horses the carrots and gently stroking them between their ears. He doesn't seem scared, but something is clearly bothering him. I can see it in his furrowed brow as I lean against the wooden door to Luna's stall, arms crossed, watching his every move.

"What's on your mind?" I can't help but ask, the curiosity gnawing at me.

North briefly glances my way before letting Pascal, the black stallion, eat the last carrot from his hand. He gazes sadly into the horse's dark eyes and shrugs. Is he hesitant to tell me, or does he perhaps just not know how to start?

I walk over and lean against the wall next to Pascal's massive head so we can look at each other. But even here, several seconds pass before North finally takes a breath and confides in me, "It's the same in here as with you and Madelyn and Grandma..."

What does he mean by that? With a puzzled frown, I stay silent, giving him the time he needs.

"When I look at the horses, I feel like I have a

special story connected to each one of them. But in reality, I can't even remember their names anymore."

His pain is so tangible, it feels like a dagger to my heart. I rush to grab some herbal treats from the burlap sack in the empty stall before returning to his side. Placing a few in his hand, I keep the last one and hold it flat under the nose of the horse in front of him. "This is Pascal," I say, my voice warm and tender. "With him, you taught me how to feed these guys without losing a finger. I was a mess at first, but your patience was otherworldly, especially with me."

As North listens, I move under Pascal's head and stand beside Calito. Gently stroking him from his forehead to his muzzle, I say, "You taught me the ropes of riding with this one. How to use my weight to hit the brakes when things got hairy." I purposefully omit the true purpose of the riding lesson. "His name is Calito, and he's the brother of that dark brown mare over there." I nod to Luna's stall, waiting for North to offer Calito a treat. He does so without hesitation. Maybe the knack for horses still flows through his veins, like driving a car.

In front of Princess and her foal's stall, I remind him of the endless hours he spent in the barn, eagerly awaiting Sunny's birth. As we approach Luna next, I recount the stories he shared with me during our intimate night together. "She's a year older than you, and your favorite horse because she once belonged to your mom. When you ride her, you feel her spirit with you, and it's like you can hear her laughter."

I give him a moment alone with the dark brown mare and fetch a jar of ointment from the cupboard. When North joins me, I tell him, "This is Symphony. She strained her left hind leg a few days ago." I step into the stall, waiting for him to follow. "She needs this ointment applied twice a day." Unscrewing the jar's lid, I offer it to North, who's just fed his last treat to the beautiful gray mare.

"What am I supposed to do with this?" Uncertainty lines his voice, though he knows exactly what I'm getting at.

"Scoop some ointment and rub it onto her hind leg, focusing on the swollen tendon."

Hesitating, North dips two fingers into the creamy paste. Squatting, he gently strokes it onto Symphony's leg, more tender than effective. "Like this?" he asks.

"No, not quite," I reply, but I can't help smiling at his careful touch. Kneeling down, I explain, "This isn't about primping for a beauty contest; it's about easing her pain. You need to apply more pressure." Without a second thought, I place my hand over his, pressing it firmly against Symphony's leg. We move in unison, rubbing the ointment deeply into her muscles. Symphony's contented snort tells us she approves. "See what I mean?"

"Yes..." North murmurs. "I see." His eyes lock onto

our joined hands.

Oh, shit.

My heart hammers against my throat, and though I should let go of him, it's as if our hands are locked together by some magnetic force. North's eyes find mine, and I'm caught in his gaze, bewilderment dancing in their depths like flames. Just one more moment, I tell myself. One more second to savor the warmth that sparked so easily from this simple touch. I gently tighten my grip on his hand, and he allows it. But his furrowed brows and piercing stare tell me I owe him an explanation for the unspoken question behind his eyes. Instead, I finally release him, the chill creeping into my palm as I do. My lips remain sealed as I stand and screw the jar back on, refusing to apologize for something so beautiful—and something he may have enjoyed himself.

A controlled sigh fills the small space around us while North continues rubbing the horse's leg. Then he, too, rises and squeezes through the narrow gap in the door. He's fleeing, I can feel it. I just don't know why, and it's tearing me apart.

The squeaky faucet in the stable's main area turns on, and I peek over the stall wall, watching North through the metal bars. He appears calm, focused, and pensive. If only I could read his thoughts in this moment.

But maybe he senses mine, or at least feels my gaze, for he tilts his head slightly toward me, reigniting the silent fire between our eyes.

A tingling sensation erupts in my stomach.

I'm the first to look away, blinking, fearful that North might see through our situation too quickly, causing everything to fall apart. I can't risk that. It's wonderful that he keeps seeking my nearness, but his eyes still hold hurt and confusion, along with a near-panicked restraint. It doesn't seem like real feelings for me. Or does it?

God, what am I supposed to do?

"What's next?" North asks, his tone more relaxed as he returns, wiping his hands on his pant legs.

"The horses go out to the paddock now." I put the ointment away, grab the ropes from the hook, and hand them to North. "You can take the two stallions." I open Princess and Symphony's stall doors and lead the mares out of the barn by their halters. Sunny trots happily beside his mom. Luna waits a bit longer, but that's okay. I have a plan.

We release the horses onto the snow-covered pasture in the breaking dawn, where they stretch their necks before heading toward the feeding trough. Greedy bunch!

As we return to the barn together, North, still holding the ropes, leads Luna from her stall. But I stop them, holding out my hand to claim the red rope he's already attached to her halter. Without question, though clearly puzzled, he hands it over.

"Grab the stool from over there," I say with a nod,

waiting for him to return with the wooden stool.

"Where do you want it?"

"Next to the horse."

North sets it down but watches me cautiously from the corner of his eye. "What's your deal?"

"Simple. You're going to climb onto Luna's back," I say, a mischievous grin spreading across my face.

"Are you insane?" North bursts into incredulous laughter. "On this behemoth? No way!" He tries to slip past me between Luna and the stall door, but I lift my arm, flattening my hand against the wall to block his escape.

"Oh, you will," I growl, locking eyes with him from just inches away.

Caught, North freezes, pressed against my arm. I can hear his breath, feel the warm wisps of it on my skin. "You're nuts," he whispers.

"Better nuts than a chicken," I counter softly, but with more intensity.

A slight tilt of our heads would bring our noses together. Silently, I dare him to do it, while he likely pleads with me internally to remove my arm. I maintain my defiant expression. Eventually, North grits his teeth, a whirlwind of thoughts racing behind his eyes, but he's not backing down. Instead, he takes two steps back to the stool.

Using the wall for support, he climbs up and grips

Luna's mane with both hands. His long legs make it easy for him to mount. I empathize with the unease he feels—I experienced the same sensation when he first ordered me onto a horse. But in the end, it was an incredible feeling and the right choice.

Luna is accustomed to her rider. She probably knows him better than he knows himself right now. While he shifts around to find the right position, she snorts softly next to me, remaining perfectly calm.

"So, how does it feel up there?" I ask, craning my neck to look at him as he stops fidgeting and adjusts his posture.

"Not bad at all," he admits, genuinely surprised, patting the mare affectionately on her neck.

"Just wait. It gets even better," I promise, leading Luna by the rope through the tall barn door and outside. North leans slightly forward and ducks his head, but his newfound balance on the horse is no longer an issue.

Once we're outside, North turns his face toward the rising sun, closes his eyes, and smiles. His happiness is contagious, and I can't help but grin as I lead Luna to the paddock, stealing glances at North over my shoulder. I open the gate and walk a few steps onto the snow-covered pasture with the horse, then ask North, "Can you get off her by yourself?"

"I think so," he answers cheerfully but makes no move to dismount. Instead, he reaches out his hand to me and gestures to the red rope. "Can I have that for a moment?"

My heart races as I realize what he must be planning. "You think that's a good idea?" My voice wavers with uncertainty.

North cocks his head with a playful smirk. "Wasn't that you calling me a chicken earlier?"

I sigh, praying my brilliant idea won't lead to disaster. Reluctantly, I hand him my end of the rope, which he holds loosely in one hand. He gently nudges Luna with his calves, and the stunning mare starts to move. At a leisurely pace, he guides her along the paddock fence, legs hanging relaxed at her sides. Then he steers her further into the pasture, without using the rope at all, and taps her belly lightly with his heels. Luna breaks into a smooth trot, causing North to tighten his legs around her, but he seems secure in his hold. Still, I can't shake my unease. Doesn't he know the risks?

"Maybe we should get you a saddle and bridle!" I call out anxiously across the pasture. He'd have better grip and control that way.

"Bridles are for beginners!" He laughs exuberantly, giving Luna another nudge with his heels, urging her to pick up speed. As they gallop together across the snow-dusted plain, my stomach clenches. He releases her mane, stretches his arms wide like an eagle soaring, and gazes at the clouds above Canada.

"North, for crying out loud!" I groan, tilting my head back and covering my eyes with my hands.

"Don't freak out!" His jubilant voice drifts toward me from across the paddock, growing closer. The pounding of hooves tells me they're slowing down, and when they finally stop in front of me, I glance up at him, relieved. Euphoric from his unique ride on Luna, he grins at me. Leaning forward, he affectionately pats her neck, bringing our faces closer. "I swear, I was born for this!" he exclaims with a freedom I haven't seen in him for ages.

I can't help but believe him.

He slides off Luna's back, unhitches the rope, and sends her off to join her friends in the paddock with a light smack on her rump. Then he takes a deep, contented breath, steps closer, and asks, "Another glimmer of hope?" His eyes search mine as if I've just handed him the world on a silver platter.

"Another glimmer of hope," I agree wholeheartedly.

North hides the rope behind his back with both hands, as if he's concealing a secret from me. Only the wind knows the thoughts he's truly hiding. "Thank you, Adrian," he says, slightly breathless. Then he flashes a mischievous grin and saunters past me, back into the stable.

"You're welcome," I whisper softly into the frosty morning air.

11. The chosen one

I trail North into the stable, where he's cupping his hands and breathing into them, likely because his fingers got chilled while riding. He slips on his fingerless gloves and stands tall like a soldier next to the ladder leading up to the hayloft. "What's next?" he asks, his enthusiasm impressive for seven in the morning.

"We need to clean out the stalls," I tell him, grabbing a pitchfork. "But I'll handle it."

His face falls in disappointment. "Why?"

I plant the pitchfork on the concrete floor and grip the handle firmly. "Because you just had a major surgery, remember? You shouldn't be doing strenuous tasks right now." He nearly gave me a heart attack earlier when he recklessly galloped through the snow. I don't even want to think about what could have happened if he'd fallen off. What was he thinking?

Pouting, but at least acknowledging his health, North reluctantly steps aside, giving me space to work. I cart the wheelbarrow into the stable and start shoveling manure out of Luna's stall while North leans against Princess's stall door, observing me the entire time. "Do you enjoy this work?" he asks at some point, making me pause and think.

As I move to the next stall, I stop in the aisle and answer honestly, "I love life on the farm. The stable work is just part of it."

He nods in understanding, but then we both glance towards the ladder, from where a pitiful meow resonates. "Oh, who's this cutie?" North coos, approaching the gray cat with white paws perched on a step at eye level with him.

"His name's Chester, and he's smitten with you," I inform him, unable to resist watching them for a few seconds, feeling nostalgic. A spark of hope flickers in me that Chester might trigger a memory in North. But nothing. I swallow my disappointment and tell North, "He's the king of this castle, although he can be quite moody."

"Aww, the stable boy calls you moody, Your Majesty," North playfully tells the cat. "He doesn't know how hard it is to keep your crown straight all day, huh?"

Just as he reaches out to scratch Chester behind the ears, the cat leaps onto North's chest. Startled, he staggers back a step, but he's already wrapping his arms around the furry bundle. "Oh my God, look, Adrian!" he exclaims excitedly, turning to me with wide eyes. "I've been chosen!"

My laughter echoes through the stable. "Yes, you've been officially knighted as the royal petter by the king himself." Leaving them to enjoy their reunion, I get back to work. The stable won't clean itself, after all. Still, I sneak glances at North, seated on the ladder now and cuddling the cat. But when he yawns four times in two minutes, I suggest he go inside and take a nap. "You didn't sleep at all last night, remember?"

Nodding, North finally rises, cradling his feline lord in his arms. As he walks past me, I ask in surprise, "What are you doing with Chester?"

"I'm taking him with me," he replies nonchalantly.

"Ruth will never let you cross the threshold with him. She's not a fan of cats in the house."

"Hmm." North pauses, striking a thoughtful pose next to me as he turns his intense gaze in my direction. He hugs the purring furball close to his chest. "Do you think she'll let me inside if I begged...*pleeease* with a cherry on top?" he murmurs, his voice seductively soft as he bats his eyelashes innocently.

I swallow hard. "That look could get you anywhere

between heaven and hell," I reply, my voice rougher than I intended, but completely sincere.

A crooked grin forms on his face before he carries the cat out of the stable, leaving me burning with the fire he's ignited between us.

Concentrating on work becomes a challenge after that tantalizing encounter. All I want is to follow him and continue the conversation, but I hold out until late morning. When I'm finished with the necessary farm chores, I finally wash my hands and head inside for lunch. As soon as I cross the threshold, however, a startling scene greets me in the living room that mercilessly steals my heart.

North is sprawled out on the couch, his cheek resting on a pretty blue floral pillow. His chest rises and falls with even breaths, his face serene, eyes closed, as he tenderly holds the sleeping cat in his arms.

Of course, Ruth couldn't deny her grandson's request. Not even the devil himself could have resisted.

A soft clatter of pots and pans drifts from the kitchen as I approach North and carefully sit on the coffee table. For minutes, I simply admire his beautiful face. The demons in his head must have finally been silenced, allowing him to slip into the realm of dreams. It's about time.

I grab the woolen blanket Ruth made for me from the backrest, unfold it, and gently lay it over him. Chester purrs for a moment, and North sighs contentedly. "Adrian...?" he murmurs sleepily, without opening his eyes, sending a jolt through me.

"Hmm?" I hold my breath as a few seconds pass in silence. Maybe North has drifted deeper into sleep, so I just exhale quietly.

But suddenly, his voice comes from far away, "I just wanted to know if that's you."

A shiver runs up my spine. I rest my elbows on my knees and bury my face in my hands. *God, North! What are you doing to me?*

When Ruth appears in the kitchen doorway, ready to call us for lunch, I quickly turn to her with a finger to my lips and gently shake my head. Today, lunch will be just the two of us.

North sleeps the day away like a baby, catching up on more than just one night's sleep. Who knows how long his inner turmoil has truly kept him awake?

I'm immensely grateful that he's found the peace he's needed for so long, and I can't bring myself to wake him. Not even in the evening when Ruth heads to bed, and I retreat upstairs. I turn off the living room light and leave him and Chester alone on the couch. A sketch of this endearing scene finds its way into the light blue sketchbook that night—right behind the picture of him on Luna this morning.

Time passes, and I finish the drawing, but sleep

eludes me. A soft knock on my door around eleven has me stirring alert. I've been wondering if I'd see him again today. Maybe that's why I'm still wide awake.

"Come in," I call from the bed, setting aside my phone after scrolling through Instagram for the past half hour.

Silently, North steps into my room, cradling the fluffy gray cat in his arms. Their eyes twinkle in the dim lamplight as he pauses near the door.

"Chester's still here?" I whisper, grinning as North resembles a drowsy five-year-old hugging his favorite stuffed animal. "Shouldn't you put him out by now?"

"No!" he retorts but instantly softens his tone. "He wants to stay."

Just then, Chester emits a pitiful meow. I arch an eyebrow playfully. "You sure?"

"Yes. He's just hungry."

"There's plenty of mice in the barn."

"He doesn't like them." North lets the cuddly furball nuzzle his chin and shoots me a mischievous look. "He prefers a sandwich."

Considering North slept all day, I can see where this is headed, and I can't help but smile. "Let me guess..." Rising from the bed, I approach them. "Roast beef with lettuce and peanut butter?"

His lips curl into a delighted grin, negating the need for a nod.

I pet Chester's head, allowing my fingers to graze North's neck in the process. It's subtle, but the electrifying moment sends a shower of tingles through me. "Alright, I'll join you on one condition," I tease.

His eyebrows knit together as we both head out into the hallway. "Which is?"

"You eat what I put on your plate."

"Hmm." North ponders, biting his lower lip. "Another experiment?"

"You could say that." We turn the corner and descend the stairs side by side. "It's called peanut butter and jelly."

Reaching the bottom, my stare determined, I take Chester from his arms and carry him to the door. "Hey, what are you doing?" North protests and watches me sadly as I let Chester out onto the porch.

"He's been inside all day. Unless you want him making a mess in your room tonight, give him a break," I reply.

"How am I supposed to sleep now?" North's pout is just adorable.

I inhale deeply, fighting the urge to wrap him in a tight hug as I walk past him into the kitchen. "Go shower, get in bed, and watch TV until you drift off," I suggest firmly.

While I prepare a classic American PB&J sandwich in Ruth's cozy kitchen, North stands beside me, his gaze locked on mine. "Are you coming, too?"

My throat tightens, and the jar of rich, dark jam slips from my grip. "To the shower? Are you bonkers?"

North snatches the runaway jar, giving me a baffled look, as if I'd just wounded his inner child. "*You're* bonkers." He sets the jar back on the counter. "I meant to watch TV."

Oh, for crying out loud!

I roll my eyes behind closed lids, admitting to myself that I'm steadily losing it. "Just sit down and eat," I send him off, then I pivot, catching my breath as he settles down behind me.

For the next couple of minutes, he quietly observes me until I regain enough composure to meet his gaze. Then I serve the food. Naturally, I double the portions because there's no way I'm letting him eat alone. I put down a plate before him and another across the table, where I lower onto my usual seat.

With suspicion, North pries apart his sandwich, eyeing the mingling of berry jam and caramel-hued peanut butter he's expected to enjoy. Any hint of innocence vanishes from his face. "Gross, Monterey," he gripes in a commanding tone I haven't heard in a while. My stomach flutters—it's the tone he'd often use when he was vying for my attention. A shower invitation wouldn't have been that far off, after all.

My cheeks warm at the memory.

"You roused Dr. Frankenstein in the dead of night," I shoot back. "What did you expect?"

North rolls his eyes, chuckles, and gives the peanut butter-jelly masterpiece a fair shot. I can't help but watch him closely, eager to see his reaction. And it's positive! The sandwich doesn't set off any gag reflexes. In fact, his face lights up with pleasant surprise. "Wow. This is really good," he mumbles through a mouthful. I know he's just saying that because I've already acclimated him to peanut butter, but after these last couple of nights, it's not a surprise anymore.

"Of course! Did you doubt me?" I finally take my first bite, and it tastes like a blast from the second-grade past.

North shakes his head, chewing contentedly. "I would never."

"And which do you prefer? Peanut butter with jelly, or with roast beef and salad?"

"I'd have to try the other one again, you know," he teases. "For a direct comparison."

"Of course." Laughing, I stand up to make us another round of sandwiches, which we scarf down at the kitchen table like it's our final feast. "Up for another experiment tomorrow?" I ask between bites.

"Why not?" North shrugs nonchalantly and grabs a drink. "What do you have in mind?"

"Since you nailed both car driving and horseback

riding, I'm curious if ice-skating still runs in your veins. If you're game, we can hit the lake tomorrow afternoon and put that theory to the test."

His face instantly lights up, and that childlike sparkle returns to his eyes. "Yes, please!"

"Make sure you catch some Z's tonight then and don't snooze the whole day away tomorrow," I tell him as I gather our plates and load them into the dishwasher. Then we both head upstairs, and I bid North goodnight in the hallway. But in that instant, he yanks me into his room so suddenly that I nearly stumble over my own feet. "What's up?" I blurt out.

He leaves me standing in the center of the room and heads to his closet. "You said you wanted to watch TV with me."

Did I?

"Make yourself comfortable and pick a movie," he directs me as he vanishes with an armload of clean clothes. "I'm gonna shower."

He must have misconstrued something about my earlier suggestion. But the fireflies in my stomach couldn't care less. They're throwing a party.

I plop down on his bed, snag the remote, and channel-surf until I land on *Jurassic World.* Can't go wrong with that one. The program preview says the sequel will follow, so that should keep us occupied for the next few hours.

Donning light blue jeans and a white tee, North returns in no time and perches on the mattress wordlessly. A déjà vu from the night we watched the hockey game together sweeps through the room, but I'm certain it only hits me, leaving North unscathed. He crosses his bare feet on the bedspread, and a frosty-fresh scent from his damp hair wafts my way, elevating our upcoming movie night into a genuinely immersive experience. Drawn in by his mere presence, I suppress a sigh because the guy beside me is way more captivating than the dinosaurs on the screen.

"Have I seen this movie before?" North inquires, eyeing the TV.

"No clue," I mumble.

"What's up, then?"

"What do you mean?"

Still riveted to the movie, he briefly licks his lips with the tip of his tongue. "You've been staring at me for two minutes straight." Only now do his eyes slowly blink and drift to mine, studying me with such a challenging silence that it sends shivers down my spine.

At first, I'm speechless and swallow the parched dryness in my mouth. I also feel my face heat up, but I can't bring myself to look away. After a moment, I finally manage to clear my throat and confess, "Sorry. You just look like..." I exhale a long, battled breath. "We've watched TV together in your room before. A few weeks ago."

Without budging, North calmly asks, "What did we watch?"

"Hockey." It's so easy to lose any grip on reality in the depths of his eyes. He's not only stealing my voice but slowly my sanity as well. "Nashville versus Toronto."

For a peculiarly velvety moment, his gaze drifts from my face, down my body, and leisurely back up. "And who won?"

"America..." I whisper, the word barely audible.

In that entrancing moment, North and I are suspended in time, and all I can feel is my heart pounding. That is until a loud dinosaur roar sounds from *Jurassic World*, and we both blink and snap out of the moment. And just like that, it's gone.

North clears his throat and refocuses on the screen. I force myself to do the same, which is incredibly difficult because it feels as if fiery shackles have wrapped around my neck, due to all the unspoken words still trapped there. After a minute, I puff out a long breath, and my left hand slides from my stomach onto the mattress.

North's hand is also there.

It's only the outer edges of our pinkies touching but...he doesn't pull his hand away. And I revel in this tiny, beautiful connection with a sense of yearning. I couldn't care less about what Chris Pratt and his red-haired friend do on Isla Nublar for the next few hours. My personal movie is playing elsewhere.

Around 1:30 AM, however, my eyelids grow heavier, shutting more and more often. I try to stay awake because I want to savor every moment with North, but the fight is futile. Sleep engulfs me in waves, making me feel as if drunkenly riding a roller coaster. Eventually, I yield and sink deeper into the pillow. There, I roll onto my stomach and let North continue watching alone.

In a heartbeat, I feel him stir beside me, and then I'm cocooned in warmth. North silently drapes his blanket over me. With my eyes shut, I'm aware of the overhead light clicking off, leaving only the TV's flicker to paint the room in soft hues. He even turns down the volume, letting me drift away effortlessly.

I want to thank him, but all I can manage now is a faint smile into the pillow, as I'm already floating beyond reach. It'll have to wait until tomorrow.

Throughout the night, my dreams are filled with dinosaurs gobbling up cats and colossal stacks of peanut butter sandwiches, gift-wrapped and left on the porch. North is absent from my dreams, even though I spend the whole night searching for him in the house.

When I finally blink my eyes open, sunlight is already pouring in through the window, and someone is bustling about the room. Half-asleep, I experience a strange déjà vu. It takes me back to the hospital when my fairy godmother tiptoed through the ICU, and all I could do was watch her silently. This time, though, it's not a girl in a yellow T-shirt who holds my attention, but North, dressed in heavy black skater pants and a matching hoodie, his back to me. He's not a good fairy, but a dark angel who stole my heart a few weeks ago.

A contented sigh escapes me as I lie face-down on the pillow, and North glances over his shoulder at me. "Good morning," he says with a warm smile.

"Hey," I mumble, relishing the snug warmth of the bed under the blanket for a little longer. It takes me a moment in my groggy haze to realize that I've overslept. "Crap!" How did that happen? And where's my phone? I prop myself up on my forearms, utterly disoriented, scanning the room until I remember that I didn't bring it last night. Damn it! I groan and collapse back into the pillow. "What time is it?"

"Nine-thirty," North reveals nonchalantly, strolling over. "Horses are ready, and the fire's crackling in the oven." He peels off his hoodie and carelessly drops it to the floor. Underneath, he's wearing yesterday's white tee, which has ridden up a bit during the impromptu striptease.

I can't help but sneak peeks at his exposed skin from behind my pillow, my mind racing in countless directions. What's he up to? Is he climbing back into bed?

North flops face-first onto the mattress beside me, sending a shiver through my body. He snuggles his pillow, resting his cheek on it, and those mesmerizing deep blue eyes flicker sleepily in front of my face. I hold my breath, spellbound, afraid the fireflies in my stomach will burst out through my nose.

He blinks slowly. Once. Twice. And then graces me with the sweetest smile morning has ever known. "Your turn," he murmurs, and since we're so close, I can feel the warmth of his words on my lips. "But wake me up for lunch, yeah? I wanna hit the lake this afternoon." With the next blink, his eyes stay shut, and his long black lashes lie still against his skin. "Oh, and your phone's on the desk." Barely conscious, he thumbs over his shoulder. "I turned it off when it buzzed at five in your room."

Speechless, I keep staring at North's face across the pillow. My heart races, urging me to reach out and brush that single strand of hair away from his forehead, caught in his eyelashes. His breathing deepens, and his face relaxes into a serene, tender expression.

I can't believe he did it. That he ventured out to the stable in the wee hours just so I could catch some extra sleep in his bed.

As North slumbers before me like a fallen angel, a thousand reasons flood my mind why I should pull him close and hold him tight against my heart. Only one reason speaks against it.

Because he doesn't remember what we were.

It's too soon for the truth. Way too soon. I don't

want to court disaster by being too hasty. But when he lies before me like that, my self-control is stretched to its limits.

Gently, I tug the blanket, as warm and inviting as a campfire, over him. His dreamy murmurs give me permission to indulge, just for a second, in the illusion that we're lying together under this blanket like nothing's changed and that horrific accident never happened. But reality intrudes, and I cautiously slip out of bed to tackle my chores. I need to be done by noon.

Because after that, I've got a date with North.

12. Because you can't

"Let's hope the ice holds," North mutters, cautiously scraping the lake's surface with the edge of his skate. "Has it been cold enough lately?"

I finish lacing up the gray-white skates he gave me before Christmas and glance up to see him cautiously navigating the trunk of a willow tree, its branches encased in ice. I didn't even have to wake him today. When I got home at noon, he was already up, helping Ruth set the table.

"It'll hold, trust me," I reassure him. January saw temperatures dip to twenty below. If the lake isn't solid now, nothing will make it so. "And for the third time— quit clinging to the tree!" If he's as nervous as I was on my first outing, our dreams of an ice hockey prodigy might be shattered.

"Then what do I hold onto?" he grumbles, eyes glued to his feet.

Now that I'm ready, I glide over and wordlessly extend my hand, stopping just far enough away that he has to stretch a bit to reach me. As North's gaze shifts from my hand to my eyes, I can almost hear the whirlwind of thoughts about our friendship churning in his mind. Especially after last night's odd TV session. And right now, all I want to do is take his hand and skate across the ice with him. But as soon as he lets go of the branches and takes a shaky step toward me, I slide back a few inches, just far enough for him to miss.

"Hey!" he complains, snapping his hand back and pouting. Now he's too far from the tree for support, which fits my plan perfectly.

"Oops, my bad. Here, let me help you," I say, moving slightly closer. But even on the second try, I don't let him grab my hand, both frustrating him and coaxing him farther from the tree.

"Adrian!" he growls. "Cut it out!" His irked expression is priceless—or maybe perfect for a sketch in a light blue sketchbook...

"What's wrong?" I taunt, offering my hand again. "Did we find something the gifted North Beckett can't master instantly? How intriguing."

"Quit it and help me!"

"I am." Grinning, I stretch out my other hand, but he continues to scrutinize me, having already seen through my game. It's no less amusing, though, as I detect determination in his eyes and know precisely what he's thinking: If he's fast enough, he'll catch me before I can pull away.

Well, North. Give it your all!

Resolve ignites his gaze, a look I've seen before, though it was about something entirely different than ice-skating. "Widen your stance," I coach him, my voice calm and steady. "And bend your knees a bit."

North follows my instructions, never breaking eye contact. Despite my warm down jacket, a shiver snakes down my spine, and echoes of his long-lost words reverberate.

I am the target...

As though we share a single thought, I feel the exact moment he takes his first genuine step. Right then, I glide back a step. He's not frustrated anymore, having anticipated it. His face now mirrors fierce resolution, like sunlight reflecting off the ice. With my hands still outstretched, I carve small arcs with my skates, left and right, steadily retreating. And North follows me across the lake.

The transformation unfolds in a mere thirty seconds. His initial steps are unsteady, but he quickly finds his balance and rhythm. After only a few yards, I have to pick up my own pace to keep us both moving. I sweep a wide semicircle on the lake, encouraging North with my gaze alone to keep up. My outstretched arms have become more of a challenge than a necessity. And as North reaches for me, he manages to grasp the tips of my fingers.

The sudden contact jolts me, costing me a fraction of my speed during my next crossover step. It's that split second that North capitalizes on, firmly wrapping his hands around mine.

The touch, so powerful and tender at once, halts the world inside me. I take a deep breath and hold it far too long, my eyes locked on his exuberant, triumphant gaze. Our steps gradually slow until we come to a stop in the middle of the frozen lake. Seconds pass. My mouth is dry, and I'm still holding his hands. Why can't I let go?

I swallow hard, trying to choke down my overwhelming emotions and pretend nothing's happened, but I can't. And when I finally lower my arms, I do so without releasing or even loosening my grip, drawing North the last few inches across the ice toward me. Up close.

Far too close...

By now, even North senses we've slid into a significant predicament, and he breathes my name soundlessly. That one word on his lips is a question, a cry for help, a warning. But I can't respond. Everything about him is magnetic.

My breath comes in gasps as I lean my forehead against his, our noses aligned side by side. I have to close my eyes, unable to endure the deep blue when so much of us got lost in there.

"Adrian—" His plea is for me to release him. I hear it in his voice. "This isn't a good idea."

Of course, it's not a good idea. No one has told North yet he's actually into guys, not girls. And I should have never come to the lake with him.

But now it's too late. We're here. And I still can't let go.

All I have to do is tilt my head a few degrees, and my nose brushes his, feeling his breath on my lips. Though North has barely moved, he gasps shakily, "Please...don't do this."

His mouth is so close to mine that barely a whisper could fit between us. I can sense every movement of his lips. They're a devilish temptation, an unholy invitation to a kiss neither of us was prepared for. And what angel could resist such a lure?

"Why not?" The aching words barely escape my lips as a hushed breath.

North's trembling exhale dances over my skin, and within it lies a truth that shatters my heart. "Because I need you as a friend... And I don't want to lose you because of this."

North doesn't dream of us as I do. He would turn

away if I kissed him now, for he feels nothing for me. Of course not. I'm the only one here madly in love. And all the little things, the moments he sought my closeness...I have misinterpreted them out of my desperate hope that we could dive into eternity together once more. I have been blinded by my own feelings. What a fool I am!

I swallow hard and release his hands. Then I try to take a calm, deep breath, and finally turn away from him. Without waiting, I head back to the shore where our boots are.

"Adrian?" His anxious, almost pleading voice follows me. But my throat is painfully tight. I don't think I could utter a single word in the next few minutes.

Sitting down in the snow, I change my shoes. It doesn't take long for North to lower beside me, silently untying the laces of his skates. From the corner of my eye, I see his questioning gaze repeatedly drifting towards me, but what's even worse is that I can also feel it.

As soon as we're both finished, I grab the heavy ice skates by the blades and head for home. North walks silently beside me, and I don't miss the hopeful looks he gives me, waiting for a reaction.

Back at the farm, I leave the ice skates on the porch and fetch my keys from my pocket. The rusty old pickup truck isn't in the yard, so Ruth isn't home. She did mention at lunch that she would go shopping in town today. As I turn the key in the lock and grab the door handle, North places his hand on mine and stops me. His fingertips are icy cold. He presses himself against the door with his back and fixes me with a gaze I can't return right now.

"Are you mad at me?" he asks so cautiously that my own guilt feels like a searing lance through my chest.

"No," I manage to croak, sounding like nails on concrete, and look evasively at our hands. Eventually, I open the door anyway and squeeze past North into the living room. I kick off my untied boots and flee up the stairs.

North follows me without taking off his shoes. "Why are you avoiding me then?"

I don't want to answer him. And I don't want to have these wretched feelings for him right now, either. Why can't it all just stop? Storming into my room, I slam the door behind me, but not fast enough. North stops the momentum and enters uninvited. Dead end. I can't escape him in here. Distraught, I cross to my desk and lean on the back of the swivel chair to find some support in this devastating situation.

"Adrian...?" His voice is so gentle behind me that my knees want to buckle. And he comes even closer. Almost tenderly, North squeezes my forearm, and yet I know that this is only the desperate cry for a friendship he so urgently needs right now. "Why won't you look at me anymore?"

A sketch lies before me on the table, a portrait I'd drawn of him weeks ago. It was after a similar lakeside encounter that feels like a lifetime ago. My chest feels as if it's fracturing into a million pieces. And North spots the drawing, too. His gaze flickers between the angelic warrior and his own hands. Today, he's donned those black fingerless gloves again, the ones he discovered in my room last time, and it's only a matter of moments before he connects the dots.

He draws in a quiet breath. "Because you can't—"

No. I can't.

The room falls so quiet that I can hear his stunned gulp. His hand slowly retracts from my sleeve. "I'm not the only one who lost something in the accident," he murmurs. "Am I right?"

My nails dig into the chair's backrest, my knuckles turning ghostly white.

"What did you lose, Adrian?" North demands, the shock draining his voice of strength. He already knows.

With every ounce of courage, I force myself to turn my head toward him, but it feels like an eternity before I manage to meet his gaze. "You," I choke out the word, barely a whisper.

There are countless ways North could have reacted at that moment. He could have placed his hand comfortingly on my shoulder. He could have hugged me. He could have told me he understands and that everything will be okay. But what he actually does sends my entire world plummeting into darkness.

He takes a step back. Away from me...

Terror flickers in his deep blue eyes. It's not just my world imploding, but his as well. "I knew you were into me. Before the accident," North rasps, his voice barely audible. "Before I lost my memories. I knew what you felt for me...because I felt the same for you, didn't I? Because we—"

As he suddenly stops, silence stretches between us, and I finish the sentence for him. "Because we were a couple. Not for long, but we were sure we'd have a lifetime together."

"Together," he echoes the word and nods, as if the thought has carried him away. But then he starts shaking his head, at first gently, then more vehemently, his eyebrows furrowing. "A couple—" It takes an agonizingly long time before his gaze refocuses on me. "But I'm not— That's impossible."

"Is it?" After all the time we've spent together these past few days...as often as he came into my room and sought my nearness over and over again. That has to mean something, damn it! I don't want to believe it's not true.

And then there's that brief moment when his eyes soften, and I can see his heart behind them. It lasts only a heartbeat, not even two seconds. But it was there. North knows those feelings were inside him. And I'm sure he sensed a part of them these past few days, even if this truth now crushes him with the relentless force of an avalanche.

In the blink of an eye, confusion floods his eyes, and he whispers, "What about Madelyn? Is that why she broke up with me? Or did I break up with her—?"

Now's the time to spill the truth. I take a shaky breath and let it out, feeling the weight of it all as I run both hands through my hair, pushing it back. "She wasn't really your girlfriend."

"What do you mean?" His voice is barely a whisper, forcing me to read the words from his lips. "There're those photos of... You two said—"

"Maddie always knew what was going on inside you. You took those photos as a cover because you hadn't told your friends at college." With my fingers laced behind my neck, I lean my head back, staring at the ceiling, searching for guidance. "You pretended she was your girlfriend so no one would ask questions."

An agonizing silence stretches on as North absorbs the information. He's gone pale. "So, I'm into—?"

Guys? "Yeah."

"And we're—"

Together? "Yes..."

As I fully face him, North backs away, bumping into the wardrobe door. Dazed, he presses his palms to his temples and digs his fingers into his hair. "And when were you planning on telling me?" he shouts. "Maybe when I would've been begging Maddie for a second chance?"

"I don't know!" I shake my head, shattered. "Your doctor warned us not to confront you with a relationship too soon. He said it would only hurt you."

North rubs his face with both hands.

"Then that night, you found the photos on your phone, and we just didn't know what else to tell you."

He lets his arms drop, taking in ragged breaths as if the room's air supply isn't enough for both of us. His eyes dart around, searching for something—for support, for a solution to the vast chasm that's opened up between us. But he finds nothing, so his hardened gaze returns to me, and he clenches his hands at his sides. "So, you all lied to me?" he asks, his voice icy, betraying no sympathy for our desperate situation. The chill it carries is something even Canada had never known before.

The sound of my loud swallow fills the room.

"I woke up with no memory, starting to rebuild my life," he snaps, edging closer with each word. "And you let me build it on lies?"

When I feel the edge of the table press into the back of my thighs, I grip it tightly, needing the support. "I'm sorry."

"What else was a lie then?" he hisses, mere inches from my face. "Is Ruth not even my real grandmother? Was I adopted from the circus as a kid?"

"You know that's not true," I mumble weakly, my

gaze falling to the floor, unable to face him any other way.

"Really? How the hell am I supposed to know that?" His furious breath scorches my skin. Right now, I'm grateful Ruth is away, since North's booming voice threatens to shatter the entire house. "So far, everything you've told me feels like one huge lie!"

"Not everything—" My voice cracks. "Just the thing between you and me."

"*Just?* This isn't some damn trivial matter, Adrian!"

I squeeze my eyes shut, but it doesn't shield me from the impending disaster. "I know..."

"You don't know a goddamn thing!" His words slash through the air like lightning, striking me square in the chest. A second later, the door slams shut, leaving me isolated and forsaken in my room.

My heart hammers against my ribs as the silence outside suffocates my senses. Overwhelmed, I crumple to my knees, arms dangling uselessly at my sides. I fixate on the closed door. Minutes pass...maybe even hours.

Jesus Christ! What have I done...?

*

It's already past eleven, and I'm sitting alone on my bed. North hasn't tapped on my door tonight to offer me a peanut butter sandwich. He skipped dinner and didn't fetch the cat from the barn, either. Since the catastrophe this afternoon, he's been sequestered in his room, refusing to face anyone. He just told Ruth he wasn't feeling well. Headaches. But I know the truth. And the pain runs so much deeper.

Maddie and I wounded him beyond words. We both shattered the already fragile world beneath his feet. No. Not us. It was me. Me alone. Because on the ice, I let my emotions overpower my reason. It was just too soon. I wrecked everything. Everything we've been building together, brick by brick, over the past few days.

But North was right about what he said. It was all just a lie. A foundation of desperate excuses and half-truths that no one should have to construct their second life upon. We heeded the doctor's advice. But none of us considered the aftermath. Or what it's like to have your own vacant memory crammed with bullshit that only muddles things more than they already are.

Resting in my lap is the powder blue sketchbook. It's been there for over two hours, though I've long since laid down the pencil. The book has thirty-five pages. Twenty-one of them hold drawings of North and me. Twenty-one memories. For twenty-one fireflies. Bittersweet moments that have shaped my world these past few weeks. The final sketch I drew today captures North and me just before a kiss on the frozen lake, the ice fracturing beneath our feet. The world we stood on is shattered. And I don't know how to mend it for him or myself.

Late in the afternoon, I called Sandy and confided in her about today's incident. I just needed to talk to someone. She advised me to give North time to process everything and not to lose hope just yet. But it's not easy. I pray Sandy's right, that he'll emerge from his room tomorrow morning and grant the world—and me—a second chance.

Honesty has to be our policy now. No more lies, no more dodging the truth. I'm done with all the secrets, the weight of them crushing my soul. It's time to clear the air and make room. A fresh start for North and me, painting our lives with new memories together. But to do that, I have to face the past head-on. My past, at least. North can't remember it anymore.

Letting out a heavy sigh, I close the sketchbook, climb out of bed, and wander into the hallway. A soft glow spills from under North's door. My heart races as I gulp in two deep breaths and creep forward. Then I give the door a gentle rap and ease it open just a smidge.

North is hunched over his computer, looking as if he finally cracked that stubborn password. He shoots me an icy glare, his face all granite, his eyes slicing through the dim lamplight. "What do you want, Adrian?" he growls, his tone sharp enough to cut.

He's still pissed. His stiff posture screams *stay away*, but I swallow my fear and inch across the threshold. I'm here now; can't just turn tail and run.

"I've got your Christmas present," I murmur, clutching the book to my chest.

His eyes flick to the sketchbook, something glimmering in those dark depths, but it's gone in an instant, replaced by that same icy mask. "Keep it," he snaps. "I don't want it." He swivels back to his computer, dismissing me.

...And what we used to be.

My chest constricts, making it hard to breathe, and my throat burns. "I'm so sorry," I whisper, knowing he can't hear or see me.

Tentatively, I place the sketchbook on his desk. "This is our story. You would have loved it, once."

He glances at it, and a spark of hope ignites in me. But I don't linger, waiting for a second chance to leave.

"Good night, North," I rasp, exiting his room.

Sleep's a cruel tease that night, a whirlwind of emotions tearing me apart from the inside. Longing. Hope. Fear. They all claw at me, dragging me back to when North was comatose, his heartbeat the only sign of life.

Drained, I start my chores the next day. Chop wood, haul it to the living room, stoke the fire, and let the horses out. But before I dive into stable work, I want to wrap my hands around a warm cup of coffee, a morning ritual as the sun creeps higher, and head to the kitchen. Normally, Ruth's bustling around, prepping lunch. Today, though, she's sobbing at the table.

My breath catches as I spot North sitting across from her, gripping her hands tightly, but neither of them utters a word.

"What's going on?" I choke out, rooted to the spot between the living room and kitchen, my heart plummeting into my gut.

Only now does North let go of his grandma's hands, rise, and swivel towards me with a deliberation that screams trouble. His face is just as unyielding as it was last night, although I could have sworn he was softer with Ruth just seconds ago. "I'm going back to college," he announces.

Wait. "What?" The confusion slips out before I can process his words. "Why?"

"I've been thinking a lot, and I—" He inhales deeply, as if steeling himself. "I need some neutral ground."

What does that even mean? I press my hand against the archway's wall, feeling as if the entire farm is quaking around us.

"I know you guys mean well," North says coolly, yet detached, "but I can't handle the pressure here anymore.

174

You think I don't see how you all hold your breath every time you share something from the past, hoping I'll remember."

"That's not—" True? But it is. So I choke down the rest of my retort.

"It's just too much," North whispers icily.

Then it smacks me like a freight train. I've smothered him. With my hope and impatience. And giving him that sketchbook last night only made it worse. I gnaw my lower lip until I taste blood. Out of all my screw-ups recently, that was the pinnacle.

North lets me absorb this reality, but his eyes hold another unspoken accusation—one that Ruth doesn't need to overhear.

He doesn't trust us anymore. Especially not me.

"Yesterday, I called some people from my contacts," he informs me matter-of-factly, like it's just a routine handoff. "I'm moving back into the dorm for now. I'll attend some classes and hope I can end the year on a high note." He hesitates and averts his eyes for the first time. His voice grows gentler. "We'll see what comes next."

An icy dread floods my veins. He doesn't plan on coming back home. Not for weekends, not for breaks. Not until he remembers his real home. That's why Ruth is weeping so bitterly. She's losing her grandson, just like she lost everyone else in her family.

And it's all on me.

My heart feels like it's barely beating.

"So when are you leaving?" I ask, though I already know the answer. North's got his jacket on.

"Now."

The word slams down like a thick barrier between us, severing the story that was ours. He leans down one last time to plant a goodbye kiss on Ruth's gray hair. Then he snatches up the black sports bag, waiting beside his chair the whole time, and strides towards the door. "Take care, Adrian," he murmurs in passing, without looking at me.

Utterly dumbfounded, I pivot in slow motion and watch him leave until he vanishes onto the porch. The door shuts behind him with a hushed click. That click sends tremors down my spine.

No, no, no, no, no!

As if jolted from a spellbinding dream, I bolt through the living room, fling the door wide, and dash onto the porch. North is already slamming the trunk shut of the black BMW we picked out together just days ago. I halt on the creaky wooden boards, aware he's seen me, but he's now deliberately avoiding my gaze. Panic surges through me, stealing my breath.

"You can't just bail like this!" I plead, gripping the support pillar. This can't be happening!

"You're dead wrong," he retorts, his voice as soft as the hush before a tempest, already yanking open the driver's door. His jaw is clenched in a tight line.

This goodbye is eerily reminiscent of the morning after our first kiss when I had to get in a car and drive away. But North had made a promise back then. A promise that seems to have evaporated from his memory.

"You vowed you wouldn't forget me!" I exclaim, desperation from the past few weeks bleeding into my words. "You *swore* it, damn it!"

"That was in a different life," is all he says.

Not for me. My hands quiver against the wood. My throat constricts, and my vision blurs with unshed tears that I furiously blink back. "You introduced me to this world! And now you're just gonna split? That's not fair, North!" I shout into the biting wind that whistles between us.

In a flash, he pivots, leaps up the porch steps, and closes the distance between us with such ferocity that I instinctively back away until the house wall halts me. "My life ain't fair either, Adrian!" he roars in my face. His expression darkens like a predator poised to strike, and he slams his fist against the wall beside my head. The impact makes me flinch, but our eyes remain locked in a smoldering struggle for the truth. "You lied to me! You, of all people!"

"I'm sorry," I choke out, my throat raw. I wish he could feel the weight of my sincerity, but not even a tank could breach the fortress he's erected since yesterday.

"I don't give a shit!" he spits, venom lacing his words. He whirls around and stomps back to his car.

All I can do is struggle to breathe through the crushing ache in my chest as I watch him slide into the passenger seat and speed away, leaving me behind. It's over.

Our story has reached its bitter end.

North has abandoned the farm. He's left Ruth. And he's left me.

Surrendering to fate's cruel hand, I crumple onto the porch steps and bury my face in my palms, as a shattered sob escapes my lips.

I don't regret many things in my life. Only three, really. That I didn't hug my dad longer the day he died. That I lashed out at my mom, calling her a lousy mother when I was thirteen. And that I didn't tell North how much he truly meant to me after coming out of anesthesia.

Maybe the truth would have overwhelmed him as much as it did today. But at least it wouldn't have been a lie that destroyed everything.

13. Ten steps to you

The wind gnaws at my cheeks, sending a frigid chill beneath the collar of my hoodie. I wish it were colder. Cold enough to end me right here and now.

I yearn to freeze, numb to the pain that's tormented me relentlessly for weeks. I want to rewind time. I want to tell North everything, and yet, nothing at all. I want to stop him from driving through the forest that night. I want it all to be over.

But none of it can happen, because the wind doesn't have that power. So I clench my fingers in my hair, hunch my head down further, and force a breath through a throat that barely leaves room for a whisper of air.

Then the sound of an engine and tires crunching over hard packed snow reaches my ears, and I jerk my head up. But it's just Madelyn's gray Volvo pulling up onto the porch, its exhaust fumes smothering my futile hope for North's return.

As Maddie steps out and circles the car's hood toward me, she gestures with her thumb over her shoulder and asks, confused, "Was that North driving down the road just now? Where's he off to?"

I lick the small wound I bit into my lower lip earlier and raise my eyes to her face. My own desperation is instantly mirrored as shock in her eyes, even without me having to respond.

She crouches in front of me and places her hands on my knees. "What the hell happened?"

So many awful things...

"I messed up, Maddie," I rasp.

"Messed up? What? How?"

"He knows we lied to him. And what he and I were before the accident."

Her eyes bulge in terror, and her cheeks blanch to the color of the snow in the yard. "And he didn't take it well..."

I violently shake my head.

"Where's he going now?" Her frantic voice pleads for reassurance that he just needs space and is cruising around town. But I can't give her that answer.

"To Calgary. He said he can't live with this pressure anymore."

Visibly shaken, she gasps for air and stands up. Her gaze is vacant, looking past the yard to the road. But as if she's mastered a mental switch in tough situations, her focus snaps back to me, and she urgently asks, "Where's Ruth?"

"Inside—" I stammer.

"And you left her alone? *Adrian!* Shit!" She whacks me on the head, jolting me from my self-absorbed stupor. "Pull yourself together! I get that you're heartbroken, but there are people who feel way worse than you right now!" With that, she stomps up the stairs and across the porch into the house. "Ruth?"

Oh my God! What's wrong with me?

I bolt after Maddie into the living room, my eyes locking onto her as she enfolds Ruth in a fierce embrace in the kitchen. The tiny, elderly woman's heart-wrenching sobs pierce through me.

"Whip up some tea!" Maddie commands in a steady, soothing tone as she brushes past me, her hand gently caressing Ruth's back. "Herbal tea." Guiding North's grandma into the living room, she eases her into the rocking chair. Ruth quivers so intensely that even the chair trembles beneath her.

Feeling the weight of the situation, I do my best to be helpful, regretting the pain I've caused these wonderful people. How can I ever make amends for this mess? Tea won't be enough, but it's a start.

As the water reaches a rolling boil, I pour it over a sachet of mountain herbs. All the while, I concentrate on my breathing and the rhythmic swishing of the teabag, unwilling to delve into the thoughts lurking just beneath the surface. After two minutes, I remove the sachet and stir in a spoonful of honey, just the way Ruth likes it. Then I carefully carry the steaming cup into the living room.

At the threshold I freeze, though, my throat constricting at the sight of this generous woman, shattered in her own little world. She pulls an embroidered white handkerchief from her apron pocket and dabs at her tear-streaked eyes. Caringly, Maddie wraps a plush purple blanket, fetched from the couch, around Ruth's legs.

My heart hammers painfully in my chest, the vice-like grip stealing my breath as I stand there, teacup in hand, suspended between the living room and kitchen.

I'm so sorry, Ruth! I never meant to hurt her.

As Maddie zips past me back into the kitchen, Ruth's eyes find mine, filled with the familiar warmth she's exuded since my first day on the farm. Time stands still as we share a silent moment, until a tear trickles down my cheek.

Ruth extends her arm, her wrinkled hand beckoning

me. Tentatively, I shuffle across the floorboards and approach her. I hand her the tea, but she sets the cup on the small wall by the fireplace, grasping my hand instead. I crumple beside her on the floor, wanting to apologize for everything I've done wrong. But my throat denies me the words. Instead, I press my lips to her knuckles in a tender kiss, resting my head on the blanket covering her legs. It's a relief to close my eyes for a moment, feeling her gentle fingers stroke my hair.

"I'm glad I still have you with me," she murmurs, her voice rough yet kind.

If she knew her grandson had truly fled the farm because of me, she would undoubtedly take those words back.

*

I don't know how I survived today, or when I decided to sleep in North's bed tonight. But after gathering myself during a brief, tearful moment in Ruth's embrace and returning to work, this is the first moment I truly let myself crumble under the weight of my sorrow. Clutching North's pillow to my chest, I inhale the lingering scent of Canadian forests on the pillowcase. His scent is both a torment and a comfort.

How I wish I could hold *him* right now, not just this damned pillow.

It's only been two months since I arrived in Canada, but it feels like I've already lived a lifetime here. So much has happened—experiences that will surely stay with me until my final days.

And North knows only a fraction of them.

He was my guiding light during this pivotal moment in my life—a brilliant star in a new sky. My North Star, someone who was always there when the ground shifted beneath me, knowing just what to say to give me courage for the next step. He shone through the darkest nights, guiding me home.

But the North Star has vanished tonight.

He's fallen from the sky, shattering into a thousand pieces like a broken mirror—just like North's memory. All that remains is a shard of a memory, painfully lodged in my heart.

The light blue sketchbook still lies at the edge of his desk, where I left it last night. He didn't take it to Calgary—he likely didn't even glance at it.

He also left behind his fingerless black gloves, which now sit on his nightstand, taunting me for my impatience with North. Defeated, I close my eyes and bury my face in the down pillow.

I just hope he's okay, finding the distance he needs in Calgary to sort through his life and rediscover himself amidst the chaos. I long to call him, to ask if he's alright, if he made it safely to university, if his friends are looking out for him. But I don't want to pressure him—never again. Besides, he probably wouldn't answer my call today, or for a long while anyway.

God, I miss him so much. I would give anything to hear his heartbeat again right now.

*

The first three days after North's departure are brutal. I force myself to rise each morning and push thoughts of him aside each evening, collapsing into sleep from sheer exhaustion. And in between, I often sit for hours in the hayloft, petting Chester in my lap.

Ruth calls North every afternoon, checking in on him for a few minutes. As his grandmother, it's her right. But each time she asks if he wants to talk to me, she simply shakes her head afterward, relaying his refusal.

By the fourth day, I find myself drifting through the house like a ghost, caught in a lifeless routine from dawn to dusk. I slog through my stable work, shrouded in an indifferent silence. But from day five, I start embracing this numbness, this disconnection from the world. It's probably the only reason I can still function, tackling the endless tasks that fill my days.

I can't recall the last time I smiled or tasted the sweetness of joy. Lately, I've considered cutting my stay at the farm short and returning to Oakspeak. But the thought of crushing Ruth stops me from leaving.

A glimmer of hope in this situation is the daily visits from Dr. George Alexander Valentine. His presence offers Ruth a temporary reprieve from the pain of losing her grandson. One can see the positive effects in the subtle pink hue returning to her cheeks.

Dr. Valentine usually arrives in the late afternoon. I hear the purr of his car's engine through the open stable door as I secure the stall behind Luna, the last horse I bring in from the paddock with Calito. I pull a carrot from my dark red hoodie pocket and offer it to the gorgeous mare. After a gentle stroke on her forehead to bid her farewell, I head back towards the house. However, I barely make it half a meter from the stall when a jolt of electricity surges through my body.

Someone's standing in the open stable doorway.

At first, I see only a dark silhouette framed by the fiery glow of the setting sun. But that's enough for me to recognize who's just ten steps away.

"North—" His name slips from my lips in a hushed whisper.

"Hey," he replies, his tone steady.

My heart, long dormant, springs to life and lodges itself in my throat, fluttering like a caged bird. "What are you doing here?" I barely mouth the question, my world quivering at its very core.

His hands buried in the pockets of his heavy black skater pants, North just shrugs, obviously deciding that's a sufficient response. "Can I come in?"

Into the stable? I nod slowly, taking a few seconds to swallow my disbelief. "You don't have to ask. Even if you're living at the university now, all this still belongs to you," I remind him, feeling rooted to the concrete floor. "I'm just working here."

"Mmhmm," he murmurs with a contemplative nod, as if retrieving forgotten information from deep within his memory. Hesitantly, he crosses the threshold and tilts his head slightly upward over his right shoulder. I'm not sure what draws his gaze, but it's as if the evening sun beckons him. At that instant, a breathtaking red golden ray illuminates his face, making his skin glow. It's just a fleeting moment, but it steals my breath away as North is transformed into a dazzling star, a celestial wonder once believed lost.

He turns back to me but remains by the gate, his tone casual, as if we're chatting over a mundane dinner. "Did you just bring the horses in?"

"Yes." I sense there's more to this than just discussing the horses. What's really at the heart of the matter? I squint, attempting to decipher the tiny white letters on the left side of his black sweatshirt. They're too far away to read. "Why did you come back?" I ask, just loud enough for him to hear from the stable gate.

A hush falls before North heaves a deep sigh, and Luna snorts softly beside me. I absentmindedly stroke her mane, grounding myself in this ethereal, star-kissed moment.

"Peanut butter," North finally murmurs as if it clarifies everything.

Well, it doesn't. "What?"

He licks his lips and briefly presses them together. "I live with three roommates," he suddenly divulges, as though he needs to fill me in on his life. "Did you know that?"

I shake my head.

"They're Jack, Max, and Brian. Max plays the guitar."

"Okay..." Unsure of where this is leading, I'm still drawn to the warmth of his presence after so many lonely days. His gentle voice pulls me in, step by step.

"They gave me a tour of the university, and I sat in on a few lectures for my study plan." North rolls his eyes. "Boring as hell."

He looks so irresistibly adorable with that expression that I ache to be near him. I crave his closeness, my heart hammering in anticipation. So, I take another step.

"I also got to watch my hockey team practice. Seriously brutal. I was glad I wasn't on the ice with them."

I can imagine. Anyone unaccustomed to the roughness—or unable to remember it, like him—would think twice before joining those rowdy players. After his injury and surgery, North will never again be able to participate in such an aggressive sport. My heart aches for him, even if he doesn't miss it right now.

"Last night, they took me to a party," he continues, his voice growing somber as if he's describing the sad fate of a forgotten teddy bear. "It was packed."

"Didn't you like it?" I ask, moving closer. God, I've missed him so much that every inch between us feels like a gaping chasm.

"I don't even know whose house it was!" he confesses, sounding defeated. I yearn to hold him and reassure him it's not that bad, but my arms can't bridge the gap. And so, I step forward once more.

"Eventually, all my friends disappeared with different girls. Claire stood before me. Apparently, we've known each other for a while. Or at least she knew me."

At the gravity in his voice, my stomach clenches. I feel like retching into the empty stall beside me as my mind conjures a montage of possible endings to his story. In my heart, North and I are still meant to be.

This time, I don't prod him with questions; I just let him unravel his tale. Each step is harder for me, fear clenching my chest, but the raw vulnerability in North's voice keeps drawing me in, inch by inch.

"Claire made it pretty obvious she wanted us to slip away to one of the rooms upstairs. She was attractive and sweet. Guys were all over her the whole night, even though she seemed to only have eyes for—"

"—you," I complete his sentence, scared of where this is going after his abrupt pause. North nods, his expression distant and wistful. "So, did you take her up on the offer?" The words spill out before I can stop them, and I immediately regret asking. I avert my eyes, wishing I could retract the question.

"No."

Of course.

Wait—

What did he say?

My head snaps up, and I hold my breath, unable to trust my ears. I think my hands are trembling, too.

North's face crumples with introspection. "There was this bizarre moment when it hit me that she'd be the first person I'd kiss. At least, as far as I can remember..." he adds softly, his shoulders drooping. "And suddenly, it felt so incredibly wrong. She wasn't the one I wanted..."

A buzz of anticipation ignites beneath my ribs, and I bite the inside of my cheek.

"I apologized and left the party," he recounts the sudden end to his night. "All I wanted was to go home."

"To your shared apartment?" I've already closed half the distance between us, and I tilt my head as I ask the question.

North doesn't respond. Instead, he takes a deep breath, bracing himself for the rest of his story. "This morning at five, I was sitting alone in our kitchen, unable to sleep."

My heart, heavy with longing, urges me across the cold concrete. If only I had my own room at university; then he could have knocked on my door at five in the morning, and we could have talked until sunrise.

But my heart isn't just heavy now. A part of it is pounding like mad, eager to take flight with fireflies because North is back. He's so close that I can see the glimmer in his blue eyes.

"My stomach had been churning all night, and I wanted to make a sandwich. Just a small one. To chase away that feeling..."

That feeling is homesickness, and it's not something food can cure.

As I take another step and he continues speaking, his voice threatens to crack. "But there was no peanut butter. In the fridge, there was only beer, Redbull, and cheese. How can anyone live off that?" On the verge of despair, he rakes both hands through his hair and scans the stable helplessly. "When the guys finally showed up at noon today, they said I don't even like peanut butter. But they don't know a thing about me. They don't know what I like! Or who I am! Or what I need—"

"Do *you* know now?" I whisper, my voice barely audible.

Wicked Fireflies. That's what's tattooed on his left chest. His response is raw and raspy. "Yes."

I can't help but smile, capturing his wandering gaze. If I just reached out, I could touch North. But I don't dare. Not yet... I close the remaining distance between us, squinting against the golden glow of the evening sun as it streams through the gate. It seems as radiant as I feel, knowing North is here. He wasn't interested in that pretty girl, and he wanted peanut butter. Could my wish on Maddie's shooting star long ago finally be coming true?

"So you came back for a peanut butter sandwich?" I murmur, lightly brushing my knuckles over his limp hands.

His fingers twitch in response, igniting all the butterflies and fireflies within me. Despite my evasive question, he rolls his eyes, looking adorably frustrated, but accepts the metaphor. "Yes, Adrian. A peanut butter sandwich." The weight of a cruel world that's stolen so much from him is evident in his next heavy breath. "With roast beef and lettuce, or with berry jelly, I don't care! As long as you're with me—at the table, on the bed, or even on the roof of the barn—and we eat the sandwich together."

Together.

The word washes over me, healing wounds deep within my soul.

I let the word's warmth permeate my heart until the last remnants of my fear and desperation dissipate. Then I thread my fingers through his until our hands are tightly interlocked. Touching him like this again feels like a miraculous gift. We stand so close I can feel his breath on my face, his scent of wild Canadian forests engulfing my senses. "I think we can do that," I whisper, resting my forehead against his and closing my eyes.

Joy swells within me, nearly painful in its intensity, as my personal sky becomes whole again with all its luminaries. The North Star has returned to its rightful place, shining brilliantly for me. And so, I find my way home, too. Neither of us will suffer from homesickness any longer.

"I missed you," I whisper, reveling in the freedom of uttering those words without fear.

And North whispers back, "I missed you, too."

A tingling sensation shivers down my spine, raising goosebumps on my skin. The sensation becomes a soul-deep shudder of warmth and chill, coursing through my body in exhilarating waves. It's as if every cell in me awakens from the stupor of the past few days. I savor each second of this extraordinary moment, suspended in time. At the bluff of eternity...with North.

"Adrian?" he murmurs after a lengthy silence.

"Hmm?"

"Before the accident...did we ever kiss?"

I'm sure he knows the answer. "Yes."

"And was it beautiful?"

I open my eyes to meet the deep blue of an untouched morning sky, despite the sun setting behind the farmhouse over North's shoulder. "Yes, it was. Very much so."

He nods, a resigned acceptance, as if the memory still lies dormant within him. "Will you tell me about it?"

It's a cherished memory I'd love to share. But not today. Not now. "Wouldn't you rather make a new memory for yourself?" I ask gently, my nose brushing tenderly against his.

North doesn't pull away, but instead exhales a soft, dreamy sigh. "Yes, I'd like that."

My fingers tighten around his hands, and my heart swells as he reciprocates the grip.

"Kiss me, Adrian. Please..." he breathes against my lips.

As he navigates this difficult period, finding his way back step by step, I'm determined not to overwhelm him. I'll never lie to him again, and I won't rush anything in this blossoming relationship. But right now, there's nothing I want more than to grant him this heartfelt request.

I guide his hands to my chest and tenderly place mine on his cheeks. Our foreheads pressed together, I lose myself in his mesmerizing eyes and feel my heart skipping with joy where his hand rests. "I hope you've gathered all your fireflies," I murmur against his mouth.

"What?" North utters, baffled. I gift the answer to

the fading sun and instead capture his lips, tenderly parting them with mine. A thousand stars light up my sky as I close my eyes and connect with North in the way we were always meant to.

The first brush of our tongues is pure innocence, reminiscent of that moment before Christmas in his room. But today, it's North who must fully surrender to this adventure, and I'm more than ready to catch him.

His hands snake around my chest, gripping the fabric of my hoodie. We're as close as I've longed to be, our breaths mingling, chests pressed together. His need for my nearness lures me like a siren's song. I willingly deepen the kiss, opening myself up to him. As our tongues dance, so do the fireflies in my stomach. North tastes like crisp winter nights and warm sunrises, of forgotten memories and a passionate future. He tastes like an eternity finally reclaimed, one I will never relinquish again.

Tenderly, I wrap my arms around him, holding him even tighter. The familiar sensation of his body and all he means to me floods back with such intensity it constricts my throat and nearly brings tears to my eyes. But now is not the time for sorrow, so I swallow that emotion, not allowing it to consume me. It's time to celebrate life—together.

And I am infinitely grateful for the time we've been

granted.

A long time later, we're still standing in the open barn door beneath the rising starry sky, wrapped in each other's embrace. I'd stay like this all night if I could, but the porch light flickers on as Ruth emerges from the house. She spots North's black BMW, excitedly shouts his name, and her elated gaze finds us.

That fleeting second isn't enough for us to pull away, and neither of us wants to. We slowly disentangle, but his hand stealthily finds mine again. It seems more truths lie ahead of us this evening.

However, as Ruth calls out, "Kids! Get inside! You'll freeze if you stay out here any longer!" I doubt our revelation will shock or disappoint her.

"We'll be right there!" I reply, turning off the barn light and locking the door.

As North and I walk hand in hand towards the house, he asks, "Are you going to explain the fireflies thing to me?"

Rubbing my thumb in small circles on the back of his hand, I flash him a lopsided grin. "Yes. Sometime."

14. The truth about sex and passwords

Ruth took the news about North and me like a champ. Honestly, we could've told her a meteorite wiped out half of Australia today, and she'd still be grinning from ear to ear.

She has her precious grandson back. That's all that counts.

We stayed up way past her normal bedtime, chilling in the living room, sipping tea, Fanta, and hot chocolate. Even Dr. Valentine dropped by for a bit, and Maddie came to say hi after I filled her in on today's stable drama. She needed to apologize to North face-to-face for our deception.

It had been ages since we'd had such a cheerful night at the farm. The vibe was infectious, especially for the fireflies doing somersaults in my gut.

I knew North wouldn't let me sneak off to my room after everyone finally called it a night and the house went quiet. First, I had to whip up a batch of peanut butter sandwiches for us. Little did I know what he had in store for them upstairs.

He nudges me toward his bed but lets me plop down solo while he sets the plate of sandwiches on the nightstand. I scoot to the center of the mattress, tucking my legs up crisscross, and wait with bated breath until he finally plops down beside me. But first, North fetches the light blue sketchbook from his desk. He clambers onto the bed like it's a jungle gym, forcing me to crane my neck to keep him in view. "What's the deal?" I ask, grinning.

Wordlessly, he settles down behind me against the headboard of the bed, stretching his legs out on either side of my hips. Then he eases me back against his chest and rests the sketchbook on my stomach. "Tell me our story."

"Now?" I ask, taken aback, trying to catch a glimpse of him over my shoulder.

"Yes, now. Please..."

"It's kinda long," I point out dubiously, considering it's nearly midnight. "We'll still be here when the sun comes up."

"I'm not tired," is his only defense. "Are you?"

"No, actually, I'm not," I admit. And then he loops his arms under mine and laces his fingers over my chest, like it's a done deal.

"Alright." I flip open the sketchbook to the first page, which depicts North's arrival at the farm, but I start my tale way before his vacation began. "Things were pretty rough at home last year. Actually, they've been that way for a while. My dad passed when I was young, and my mom remarried..."

When I recount the part about Maddie face-planting into horse poop, North chuckles behind me and hands me the first sandwich. He snags one for himself, and I hear him munching quietly as I keep talking, sometimes mid-bite.

Rehashing my time with North through my storytelling is electrifying. I suddenly recall so many tiny details that might have slipped through the cracks otherwise. Like the night of the hockey game when he caught me off guard in the kitchen making sandwiches, and I dropped the knife because he looked so damn good in his jersey. During our midnight ride through the snow, I could feel his warm breath on the nape of my neck. And Chester, up in the hayloft, plopped right onto North's face like his head was a treasure that needed hiding from the Easter Bunny.

I recount to him in vivid detail the period when all we could sense from him were the steady beats of his heart. The fear, the anguish, and the yearning. And how, during those agonizing weeks, I dialed his number repeatedly, pretending for a fleeting instant that he would answer, and I could hear his voice once more.

"Huh," he breathes softly behind my ear, idly tracing a finger above my navel. "That explains the four thousand missed calls on my phone when I finally turned it back on."

I'm certain it wasn't four thousand, but it was a considerable amount. And since we're discussing phones, I fish mine out from my back pocket with a swift tug and open our cherished WhatsApp chat history.

It's just a handful of lines, and North skims through them quickly. As I tilt my head back slightly, I catch a glimpse of his faint smile. "Damn. I was such a sweetheart," he murmurs, his nose scrunching up adorably, filling my heart with warmth.

"You were," I confirm, placing my hand over his, which still lingers on my stomach.

When North puts my phone away, I flip to the next page of the sketchbook. But before I can continue our tale, he whispers into my ear, "Do you know what my computer password was?"

I recall him hunched over the PC on his last night here. At the time, I figured it had something to do with his hockey team. But as North's lips teasingly graze my ear, I involuntarily hold my breath, curiosity making my heart race. "No," I admit. "What was it?"

"Adrian21. With a capital A."

For countless reasons, I gape at the dark screen of the turned-off television, then I swallow hard before asking, "How did you figure that out?"

"Actually, you guided me to it." North intertwines his fingers with mine. "I tried all sorts of combinations with *Wicked*, *Fireflies*, and the number *twenty-one*, but nothing clicked. Then you made me realize I'd been falling for you for a while, and I—" He pauses briefly, letting out a heavy sigh. "I thought back to the moment I first woke up in the hospital and saw you by my bedside like an angel. I wondered what password I'd have chosen then. And instinctively, I typed your name."

It sounds enchanting, but I can imagine how jarring it must have been in reality, especially amidst the avalanche of revelations that day.

"Did you change it after?" I inquire softly.

His chest swells with a deep inhale behind me, then

deflates. "At first, I intended to. But then I couldn't." He rests his chin atop my head. "And now I don't want to anymore."

His voice, a blend of playful charm and heartfelt sincerity, makes me grin. "Is it okay that this makes me happy?"

"I didn't tell you to make you sad," he retorts, giving my hand a gentle squeeze. Then he retrieves the sketchbook and positions it so we can both view the current drawing of him lounging with Chester on the couch. "Now keep going. I want to know how our story ends."

"You already know the ending. You penned the conclusion yourself today."

"You know what I mean!" he playfully growls. "Come on!"

God, how I've missed this stern and impatient side of him!

"Okay, okay, I'm getting to it," I laugh and then continue where we left off from our WhatsApp chat on my phone earlier. It's already three in the morning, and he's practically heard the entire story of how we met and became a couple. Only a few pages remain, but he's still eager to hear my take on everything that transpired. And I'm more than happy to indulge him.

As we reach the last drawing with only North's escape to Calgary left—about which I have little to say—he flips a few pages forward and back, impatient. "Is that it?" he inquires, almost in disbelief.

"For now, yes."

"There's room for more."

He's right. There's room for *so* much more. "Well, eternity has only just begun."

"Hmm," he hums, resting his chin on my head, the vibration resonating through my skull. "You're right. We'll likely need a few extra pages."

"Or maybe a second book."

"Yes." I can hear the smile in his voice, and I know precisely how his eyes must be twinkling. "But, um..." he begins, sounding slightly uncertain. "Have we...I mean...ever...done more than just...?"

His stammering is endearing. But he'll never finish the question by lunchtime at this rate, so I help him out, "Have we had sex?" The words, now that I consider them, sound peculiar even to me, and I squint a little, which he can't see from behind.

"Yes," he confirms my inquiry.

"No, we haven't."

"Oh."

Oh, what exactly? He makes it sound enigmatic,

leaving me unsure whether he's surprised or taken aback.

"That's good," he eventually adds, further puzzling me.

"Really?" I can't help sounding somewhat miffed. "And why is that good?"

North takes the sketchbook from my grasp, closes it, and sets it on the nightstand. He also switches off the bedside lamp and scoots back slightly to lean over me from behind. "Because there's still something we can experience together for the first time," he whispers against my lips before placing a tender kiss on them.

I inhale his presence, allowing it to mend the last remnants of my fractured heart, which has yearned for this moment throughout the past weeks. "I like that idea," I murmur softly, resting my hand on the nape of his neck and drawing him into a deeper kiss.

The summer solstice is upon us, and as I look back, I can't help but marvel at the amazing months that have unfolded. Despite North not regaining his memories, we've seized every opportunity to create new, unforgettable ones.

North completed his final semester of training through distance learning, only traveling to Calgary for a few days last week to take his exams. I missed him terribly, especially at night when the bed felt cold and vast without him. But our reunion was all the sweeter for it. And it wasn't the only one.

Sandy, Cameron, and Thane touched down in Canada two days ago, and they're spending the first week of their vacation with us on the farm. Introducing them to my boyfriend was thrilling, even if I was a bundle of nerves. Mom already met North at Easter when she came for a visit, and they quickly formed a special bond. Also Ruth and even Madelyn's mom, who's been doing so much better, instantly embraced her, so I can picture Mom visiting us more frequently in the future.

Armed with three cans of Fanta and two bottles of water, I head back outside. As the sun set, we lit a roaring bonfire in the pasture to celebrate the solstice and our accomplishments, including my acceptance into art school in Edmonton. After ending my official stint as Ruth's au pair, I've extended my stay on the farm indefinitely. It now feels more like home, a place I'm happy to tend to.

This fall, I'll start my own two-year distance learning program, which will fit seamlessly into life on the farm. The past few months have shown us how well North and I can work side by side.

Under the vast, star-studded sky, I meander across the pasture, lost in thought, to rejoin my friends. We've arranged straw bales around the towering fire, where we've been nestled for the past few hours. It feels like a giant, multi-tiered Tetris bench, with North lounging beside Thane. I can't help but grin every time he glances my way—like he's doing now. After all this time, he's still my

North Star. And he always will be.

As I join the others, I circle the fire, distributing the drinks that had run out half an hour ago. The guys wanted Fanta, Sandy requested water, and I keep the second water for myself. Maddie gets nothing, as she dozed off just before midnight. In slow motion, she leaned further and further to the side until she found a makeshift pillow on Cameron's thigh. It was a hoot to watch, and I can't wait to tease her tomorrow about spending half the night with her head in a Yankee's lap.

Cam doesn't seem to mind being a pillow. In fact, he even draped his sweatshirt over Maddie earlier when she shivered in her sleep. His hand still rests on her shoulder, and occasionally, his fingers trace small, inconspicuous circles.

Feeling the heat of the fire on my cheeks, I step back a few paces to the pasture fence instead of sitting next to North again. From here, I can easily chat with everyone and enjoy a perfect view of North behind the crackling flames. It's wonderful to be with him, but sometimes it's also nice to simply watch him from a distance. Both have their charm.

One by one, the cans hiss as the guys open them, and then we all raise our drinks to the center. "Cheers!" I shout to the group.

"To long nights with good friends!" Sandy completes my toast before everyone takes a sip.

North lowers his can, his lips pursed and cheeks puffed for a beat. His eyes mist over as they lock onto mine, the fire's glow flickering between us. He covers his mouth and nose in the crook of his arm, stifling a belch to avoid embarrassing himself in front of Sandy and the others.

The sight hurtles me back to last winter, when I'd first witnessed this endearing quirk. It held such profound meaning for me then, and now that feeling crashes over me like a tidal wave. I've lost count of how many times I've fallen for North Beckett all over again, but this moment definitely tops the list.

"Hey, Adrian! You good?" Sandy's voice cuts through my reverie. Apparently, I missed something she said, and now she's poking fun at me.

"Sorry," I say, still captivated by North. It's as if his gaze has ensnared me with an invisible tether. "I just had some intense déjà vu."

"Me, too," North murmurs, lowering his arm but keeping his eyes on me.

My heart pounds in my chest. "What do you mean, 'me too'?" That was before the accident. He shouldn't remember.

Right?

"North?" My whisper is barely audible, but he doesn't respond.

Instead, he hands the Fanta to Thane without a glance and says, "Hold this!"

A whirlwind of thoughts swirls in my head as he stands, but none of it makes sense. Time seems suspended, and everything unfolds with an otherworldly slowness.

With one step for momentum, North launches himself through the fire, tucking his legs and spreading his arms like a legendary bird in flight. His open hoodie flaps like dark wings, and the wind whips embers around him, creating a mesmerizing dance. For a split second, North isn't just leaping through the fire... He's soaring.

Like a phoenix reborn.

He lands with an ethereal grace, crouching low with his hands on the grass. A flicker of mystery dances in his eyes before he straightens and closes the remaining distance between us.

Speechless, I stare at him with my mouth agape as he cradles my face with his hands, leans in, and whispers, "How many, Adrian?"

I know exactly what he means. "Twenty-one," I whisper. The water bottle slips from my grasp, and I clutch his black hoodie instead. With him, it's always twenty-one.

"And do you know when *I* had them all together?"

A shiver races down my spine. He's asked me this question before, long ago. I know the answer, yet I murmur, "When?"

North seals my lips with his own. His kiss is tender and profound, carrying not only the promise of *forever* but also the key to his past and the memories that come with it. Overwhelmed and breathless, I cling to him with all my heart.

When he finally pulls back just enough to rest his forehead against mine, a smile settles on his lips as he reveals the truth for the second time in this life, "At the end of day one..."

Forever.

ANNA KATMORE
Unfair
LOVE

Before you close this book, I warmly invite you to take a peek into my heartfelt gay romance trilogy

CRUSHED HEARTS

A game of fast cars, safewords, and true love.

*

Slowly, I pull Sebastian's hand with the peas from my face, and both our arms lower together. "Can you please stop looking at me as if you were thinking about our last kiss the entire night?" I sigh.

He drops the pack and instead intertwines our fingers, still caressing my neck with his other hand. His eyes are a chestnut fire that burns its way right into me. My heart pounds frantically as he leans closer, inch by inch, and whispers, "Can *you*?"

Unfair Love

My world shattered when I met my match.

I pride myself on keeping control of everything. Always. My only weakness? Reckless challenges.

After losing my car to the new street racer in town, Sebastian gives me a chance to get it back. His condition: two hours in which he can do with me whatever he wants. No safeword allowed.

While I know this could very well become the biggest mistake of my life, I accept. And when he kisses me, I reach my fucking limits.

Once in a lifetime, you meet a unicorn.

Raffael is pure Nordic ice. Controlled. Determined. And drop-dead gorgeous.

Winning his car was a lucky strike. Winning his heart when he's so afraid of the truth, turns out to be the hardest challenge I've ever raced to complete.

...

"I'm thinking about a smoky skull on the hood. And maybe a skeletal middle finger for the rear."

Rolling her eyes, Tanja deadpans, "Awesome."

"Hey, we cannot cover the Corvette in pixies, even if you'd love that, baby," Felix mocks her and bumps his shoulder into hers so she loses the chicken trapped between her chopsticks. While she fishes for it again, my WhatsApp beeps with a message. I stick my chopsticks into the box I'm still holding and, with my free hand, fetch my smartphone from my jeans' pocket.

As I unlock the display, however, my pulse jumps from sixty to two sixty in a nanosecond. All sounds die in the room as I'm staring dumbfounded at my phone.

I swallow.

"Okay, dude, we can hear your heart beating over here," Felix says a little nervously. "So either you won the lottery, or—"

"Sebastian sent you a message," Tanja finishes his sentence on a joyful breath.

I look up into her hopeful eyes, my lips still

thinning.

Instantly, her smile gets wider. "What did he say?"

"Oh, come on," Felix moans at her. "Give the dude some privacy."

I usually don't mind Tanja's endless curiosity, but tonight, I actually appreciate Felix's intervention. It scares me to death that I only read his name on the display and not even the message itself yet, and still, something inside me goes crazy like I won a Lamborghini or something.

When I don't move for a lengthened breath, Felix starts to pack up the food and puts it back into the plastic bag. "It's late. We better leave."

"You want to do *what*?" Tanja's outraged protest is almost sweet as he takes the chopsticks out of her hands.

He tosses them into the bag, too. "Get up, Tanja."

"But why? It's so sweet, and I—"

Felix grabs her chin and makes her look up at him, standing above her. "Door! *Now!*" he commands and nails her with a glare that leaves no room for discussion. Whoa, even I feel the urge to rise and get my jacket to leave.

Tanja's eyes widen with surprise, then she gets up from the couch and follows him to the foyer. With me right behind her, she throws a glance over her shoulder, mouthing a confused *"What?"* at me. All I feel able to do is shrug. I haven't seen Felix like this before. But at least he's found the right tone with her to make her obey.

"We can finish eating at my place," he offers, just the slightest bit softer, yet still strict enough for her not to argue.

Tanja whirls around and kisses me goodbye on the cheek. "Call me later and tell me what he wanted," she whispers and grins before she slips out the door.

Felix claps his hand into mine. "We can speak about the airbrush painting tomorrow."

I nod. "Thanks for the food."

Then the door falls shut, and I'm alone. I turn around to scowl at my phone on the coffee table ten feet away. Holy fuck. Something's seriously wrong with me if a tiny beep can break off a cozy dinner like that.

With my heart racing once more, I walk back into the living room and plant myself on the couch, finally opening the message.

Sebastian
You know that you only gave me the key and not the papers back, right?

I stare at the single line for a very long time, feeling a strange excitement at the slight provocation in the words. Now what? Start a conversation? Just tell him to come by tomorrow and pick them up? Shit, all of those thoughts are confusing. Most of all, the fact that I even have to think about it and not just reply like I normally would with any other person in the world.

I fold my hands over my mouth and nose and blow out a nervous breath. Then I type just a single word.

Me

Yes.

It takes three seconds until the two checks turn blue, and another ten until a new text pops up. All this time, my fingers cramp around the phone.

Sebastian

Planning to change that?

Oh boy, this means meeting again. Both excitement and a flood of fear swamp me. My mouth dries out.

Me

Yes.

Three dots doing the wave indicate that he's typing something again. Transfixed, I stare at them until they change to text.

Sebastian

Great. Is yes the only word your phone spits out?

He has me grinning with that, and I type just *yes* again. But then I delete it. That's stupid. Or is it? After all, he walked into that one. While I type it again and delete it once more, the waving dots reappear. He's typing, too. His message comes in before I can send mine. Which I wouldn't have because I deleted it again.

218

Sebastian

Seriously, how many times did you type fucking YES now and delete it again?

I crack up laughing and then put three teary-laughing smiley faces before my answer.

Me

Too many times!!

Then I sink deeper into the couch, dip my head against the backrest, and grimace at the ceiling. My heart rate normalizes before his next message comes in, and I actually start to enjoy the conversation that grows a little faster from then on.

Sebastian

So... My papers, Raffael?

Me

I'll mail them to you.

Sebastian

Don't you fucking dare, snowflake...

Me

Hey! Easiest way.

Sebastian

The easiest way would be to meet me and hand them over.

I swallow at this obvious request. It wouldn't be the easiest way. If anything, it's the hardest way I can imagine. I take a long time to consider how to ease out of this.

Me

Sorry, I have a really busy week. I can't.

Sebastian

Coward

Me

I'm not. It's true. Lots of uni stuff to do.

Sebastian

Your final week before the summer? I've been to college, too. I know how it goes.

I bite my bottom lip. Fuck. There's probably no easy way out of this. But the last thing I want is Sebastian in my apartment again. So I sigh and suggest the café where Tanja told me the two of them went before that fatal night in the playroom.

Me

Fine. Meet at Starbucks down the road? Sunday at 4 pm.

Sebastian

FRIDAY at 4 pm. Good night, Raff.

Shit! I gulp. Friday is tomorrow.

...

More books by Anna Katmore

ON THIN ICE

Counting Fireflies

Splintered North

*

Seventeen Butterflies

GROVER BEACH PLAYERS

Play With Me

Ryan Hunter

T Is For...

Dating Trouble

The Trouble with Dating Sue

FALL FOR ME

The Impossible Bet

Taming Chloe Summers

CRUSHED HEARTS
Unfair Love
Broken Dawn
Awaking Trust

ADVENTURES IN NEVERLAND
Neverland
Pan's Revenge

GRIMM WAS A BASTARD
A Prince for Little Red Riding Hood
A Wolf in her Way

*

Eloyn
My Secret Vampire
You were my Fairytale
Three Shades of Sinful

"*I'm writing stories because I can't breathe without.*"

At six years old, Anna Katmore told everyone she wanted to be an author after she discovered her mother's typewriter on a rainy afternoon. She could just see herself typing away on that magical thing for the rest of her life.

In 2012, she finished her first young adult romance "Play With Me" which was the beginning of her true writing career, with many books to follow.

Today, she lives in an enchanted world of her own, where she combines storytelling with teaching, and she never tires of bringing a little bit of magic into the lives of her beloved readers, too.

Anna's favorite quote and something she lives by:
If your dreams don't scare you, they aren't big enough.

For more information, please visit www.annakatmore.com